DWELL

(Kassidy Bell Series)
Book 2

Lynda O'Rourke

First Edition Published by Ravenwoodgreys
Copyright 2015 by Lynda O'Rourke

Story Editor
Tim O'Rourke
Book cover designed by:
Tom O'Rourke
Copyedited by:
Carolyn M. Pinard
www.cjpinard.com

For Mum and Dad

DWELL

Chapter One

"I told you I was evil."

Ben Fletcher's words echoed through my head – pounded my eardrums – made me gasp short stutters of breath. As the realisation of now being trapped inside one of Cruor Pharma's vans raced through me, I knew I'd been an idiot. I'd been foolish. Why hadn't I just kept walking? Taken my chances to outrun the police down Strangers Hill. I had managed to escape the clutches of the hospital at Cruor Pharma only to now end up trapped in here with one of the doctors. As if to make myself feel better, that little voice inside my head reminded me that I'd only come back to the van because I'd heard Raven call out and Ben had said that he'd picked her up on Strangers Hill. But now, as I slowly turned my head and stared into the back of the van, all I could see was blood. No Raven – just blood, and lots of it.

"I heard her," I whispered, my eyes now falling upon Ben. He clutched the steering wheel tightly in his hands.

Ben turned his head sharply. His cloudy black eyes met mine. A chilling grin stretched across his face.

"No, you didn't," he sneered. "That was me."

Ben swung the van off the road that led into Holly Tree and sped down a narrow lane through the patchy fog. He took the bends at speed, his driving becoming more erratic. If he didn't kill me, his crazy driving would.

"Where are you taking me?" I gripped the edge of my seat as the van took a sharp left heading further away from the town of Holly Tree.

"I don't know," Ben laughed and shook his head. "I don't know what the *fuck* I'm doing". He slammed his fist down hard onto the dashboard. "I should be taking you back to the hospital. Or I could just have you all to myself." He grasped a fistful of his black hair and yanked on it. "But what I'm trying to do…" he stuffed his knuckles into his mouth and bit down hard. "What I'm trying *really hard* to do is… help you get away."

"Why would you even think about taking me back to Cruor Pharma when it was you who helped me escape?" I shifted away from Ben, nearer to the door – out of his reach. His unpredictable mood sent fear rushing through me.

"Because that is what *I* want to do but Ben keeps on fighting back," he hissed. "He always wants to do the right thing – I can't get him out of my head." He took his hands off the steering wheel and cradled his head in his arms.

The van lurched to the right – heading straight for a ditch. I flung myself toward the steering wheel and tried to straighten our path.

"*Take the fucking steering wheel!*" I screamed. "You're gonna kill us both!"

"I can't die," Ben laughed. He took the steering wheel in his right hand and grabbed me around the waist, pulling me close to him. "But I wish Ben would."

I tried to pull away from him but he held me tight. He buried his face into my hair and sighed. "I want you," he breathed, "I want to keep you – back at the hospital you invited me to go with you – remember?"

I nodded my head – too afraid to speak. The outside world was rushing toward the windscreen at a terrifying speed – I felt like I was falling from the sky – waiting for impact. I wanted to pull away from Ben – leap for the door and throw myself out. But I was still held in by the seatbelt and Ben's tight grip. If I struggled with him then the van would surely crash. I had to wait for the right moment. Wait for him to stop the van.

The radio suddenly blasted into life making me jump. It had turned on all by itself.

"Let's have some music, shall we? I love this song," Ben whispered into my ear. He sung the lyrics.

I was made for lovin' you, by Kiss filled the van. Ben began to tap in time to the music against my hip. His hand had now loosened its grip on me. I screwed my eyes shut as we took another tight bend to the right. I had no idea what crazy shit was going on inside Ben's head or even if it was him sitting beside me in the van. He kept referring to himself like he was another person – like he had been taken over by Ben, but it seemed more like the other way round. If Ben was the one wanting to do everything right then I wished he would take over the body sitting next to me. I wanted the Ben who had let me escape Ward 2 – the one who had led me to the canteen and given me the key to my freedom – Doctor Ben Fletcher with the crystal blue eyes. Where had he gone? Lost inside his own body – swallowed by another. Maybe I could release the seatbelt while the music played loudly and he wouldn't hear it. I would have to stretch a little to reach it. I turned my head slowly and looked down. *Talk to him – keep him calm,* that voice inside my head instructed me – *don't let him suspect anything.*

"Why did you help me?" I asked, my eyes

never leaving the seatbelt.

"There's something about you I like," Ben shouted over the music.

"What's that then?" I asked casually, sliding my hand slowly over the leather seat toward the release catch on the seatbelt.

"You're easy to play with," his voice lowered, his hand fell from my hip and slid down my thigh. I felt his fingers dig into my flesh and slowly stroke the top of my leg – up and down. I wanted to push his hand away but I didn't want to make him angry – not while I was trying to undo my seatbelt. I could feel myself tense as his fingers pushed further up under my hospital gown. I stretched a little further. My fingers just an inch away from the button that would free me from the seatbelt.

"Does that feel good, Kassidy?" Ben whispered into my ear. "You said you wanted me to take you – back at the hospital."

I turned to face him, my left arm still stretched out behind me – my finger now on top of the button. As I pushed down on it, my eyes met his. They were still a cloudy-black but there was something in them – something that seemed to trap me – pull me in – like a magnet. The van had slowed to a crawl. Ben's eyes were now on me and not the road. His hand had travelled higher up under my hospital gown and his touch was like electric. Short sparks of heat seemed to be going off inside my body, like fireworks exploding. He leant over to kiss me – I leant forward to feel his lips. The seatbelt fell away breaking the magnetic stare between us. Ben's eyes looked down – they followed the seatbelt as it left me free.

"You're not leaving me," Ben hissed, "*I won't let you*."

As Ben lunged forward, I lifted my legs and shoved my heels hard into his chest. I flung my arm out behind me and blindly fumbled for the door handle – my fingers frantically searching for my escape.

"*Let me go!*" I shouted, slapping him across the face as he crawled over me. His hand caught mine and he pinned it down.

"I thought I'd already told you – I want to keep you – forever." Ben smiled.

"I don't think so," I spat. "I'm not yours to keep." My fingers pulled on the handle – the door fell open. I tried to push myself out from under Ben. My head hung from off the seat and I could see the gravelled lane as the van continued to roll on. The cold morning air struck my face and stung my eyes.

.

"Kassidy, what the hell are you doing? You're gonna fall out and kill yourself." There was panic in Ben's voice as he grabbed me up and slammed his foot on the brake. "I didn't help you to escape just so you could throw yourself out of a van and die, you know."

I stopped struggling with him. My heart thumped wildly as I looked up into his eyes. As they peered down at me, a look of confusion was etched across his face. Those crystal blue eyes were back. Ben had come back.

"You were trying to hurt me," my voice trembled. "I was trying to escape from you." I flinched as he leant across me and shut the door – afraid that he would flip back into crazy mode.

"I don't remember," Ben shrugged. He looked down at his hands and shook his head slowly. "I remember you getting in the van – that's all."

"You tricked me into the van," I whispered. "You told me Raven was in here. You even spoke to me in Raven's voice and I was dumb enough to believe it." I shifted away from him. I wanted to put as much distance between us as possible.

"I'm sorry, Kassidy. I don't want to hurt you – I *really* don't. I wanted to take you far away from here and Cruor Pharma. Far away enough so Doctor Middleton could never find you," said Ben, staring out the windscreen. "I thought I could manage it – control myself but…"

"But what?" I snapped.

"I don't know," he glanced back at me, a look of sadness in those eyes. "Back at the hospital, I can control myself better – push the *real* me through, but out here – with you – I just lose myself." He buried his face in his hands. "Damn it," Ben kicked out – his foot caught the accelerator causing the van to rumble and shake.

"Don't get angry, *please*." I reached for the door handle, ready to run.

"I'm okay," Ben looked up, his blue eyes still present. "I have to get you away. You're all right – I'm in control." He reached for my hand but I snapped it away.

"In control for how long?" I asked. "I can't take that risk."

"Please, believe me. I can't just let you out here in the middle of nowhere. The police are after you, the cleaners are looking for you and if either one of them finds you… Cruor Pharma will be your next stop and final stop," said Ben, "Believe me – I'm not lying to you."

I shook my head, "You've already fed me a

bunch of *bullshit* – not just lies." I held my arm up. "You fed me with VA20. *Look at my arm*. I believed you back in Ward 2. I believed you when I got into this *fucking* van and now you want me to believe you again?"

Ben nodded his head. "You don't stand a chance out here by yourself – you have to believe me."

I knew deep down that I would never make it in time to Holly Tree if I got out of the van and walked. My ankle was still hurting – that would slow me down. I needed to get to The Fallen Star where Jude, Max, and Raven were hopefully heading for – if they were still alive. Driving far away with Ben wasn't a safe option but if I could get him to take me to the bar where Jude's car was, then maybe I might stand half a chance. I looked at Ben. Could he drive me to The Fallen Star without turning on me? Could I trust him? I had to. Time was running out and if I didn't make it to The Fallen Star then I just might miss my friends. Then where would I go?

"One day I'm gonna believe you and you're gonna kill me," I whispered. "Take me to The Fallen Star."

CHAPTER TWO

"The Fallen Star isn't far away enough for you to be safe," said Ben, glaring at me. "Why do you want to go there?"

"Because that's where I'm meeting my friends," I said, "that is if you or your *cleaning buddies* haven't disposed of them."

"I haven't touched your friends," said Ben. "I know they made it out of Cruor Pharma together. I saw them scampering down Strangers Hill. As for the cleaners, I can't say. I know they're looking for you all."

I felt a sense of relief knowing that my friends had made it out of Cruor Pharma. It gave me some hope and reassurance that heading for The Fallen Star was the right thing to do. I wanted to see them again. I didn't want to be alone like this – always looking over my shoulder – always on the run. But that sense of relief was overshadowed by the thought of the cleaners roaming the countryside looking for us. How did those shadowy creatures get about unnoticed by members of the public?

"Tell me about the cleaners, what are they?" I asked as Ben turned the van around in the lane.

He sighed, reluctant to tell me. "They are servants who clean, kill, and destroy whatever they are asked to. They are unrelenting. They won't stop until they have got the job done. Which is why you aren't safe in Holly Tree. They are monsters who will haunt your every step. You will never be free of them. You will never be able to stop anywhere for too long. The cleaners will always be following, but if you keep one step ahead of them – you can stay alive."

"So I'm not safe anywhere. Whether it's Holly Tree or the other side of the world – they will always be chasing me?" I said, staring out at the patchy fog that lingered over the empty fields.

"That's why I wanted to take you as far away from here as possible. If you keep a few days ahead of them then you stand a chance of leaving them behind, at least for a while." Ben turned the van into another lane. The wooden sign post read *Holly Tree – 4 miles*.

My heart sank as I realised that I would always be on the run. I would never be able to settle – never sleep soundly – never live a normal life.

"How can I spend the rest of my life like that?" I snapped. "A life on the run – I can't live like that."

Ben looked at me, his eyes full of regret. "I'm so sorry, Kassidy. I wish I could make it all better, but I can't. I wish I could make *you* better." His eyes fell upon the black, lumpy veins that twisted under the skin on top of my hand.

"Make me better like a normal doctor would you mean?" I scoffed. "How can you walk about parading yourself as a doctor? Pretending to be something you're not. Hiding the monster that you really are under your scrubs. How can you live with yourself?"

Ben nodded his head as if in agreement with me. "I'm not living, Kassidy. I should have been dead long ago – my life has gone on way beyond what it should have. And as for parading as a doctor – a very long time ago, I was a very good doctor – a real doctor who cared for his patients, but that got taken away from me. I wasn't given the chance to argue – I had no choice. It happened."

"But it didn't have to happen to me, did it? You could have stopped this. It's no use pulling the drip from my arm after the damage is done and then trying to help me. You know, maybe you should have just left me in Ward 2 for Howard to finish me off – at least it would be all over now," I spat.

"I know this sounds crazy, but that wasn't always me in Ward 2." Ben held up his left hand as if to stop me from butting in. "It was my body but it wasn't me making the moves. I was in there somewhere – trapped inside my head but I can't always get out. It's like a prison inside me. It snatches me away from the living and throws the key away. When the door reopens, I'm left with nothing but horror. Gruesome sights of something I don't remember playing a part of."

I leant my head against the window and curled my legs up onto the seat. The motion of the van making me feel sleepy. If Ben was telling me the truth about himself and he had no control over his actions or couldn't remember the things he did, then could I really blame him for what had happened to me? I thought back to Carly – that room where she had tried to kill me in the hospital. That wasn't really Carly – she'd had no control over herself – something else had. I glanced over at Ben. I knew I was taking a big risk letting him drive me to The Fallen Star. He could flip at any moment and then the struggle to get away from him would begin again. I tried to reassure myself that my decision to let him drive me was a good enough reason to risk sitting in this van with him. I couldn't

21

run very fast with my ankle, the police were after me, and the cleaners were hunting me like some kind of blood sport.

"You didn't tell me what the cleaners are," I said, staring at Ben. "You told me what they did. I want to know – what are they? Ghosts? They float through walls and doors – that's what ghosts are meant to be able to do – isn't it?"

"They aren't ghosts," whispered Ben, running his fingers through his black hair. He continued to drive the van along the road, his eyes constantly checking the rear-view mirror.

When he didn't offer up an answer to my question, I said, "I used a makeshift cross against them - back in the hospital kitchen. I hadn't meant to but it worked. They seemed to shrivel away."

After a few minutes of silence, Ben said, "A cross will only work for a short time. It may gain you a couple of minutes to run but if you keep using it on them, they will eventually find a way to get around it."

"How?" I asked, my fingers rummaging around in my jacket pocket – searching for the crucifix that had belonged to Father William.

Ben shrugged and shifted in his seat, "They will wait until you're asleep – unprotected – unguarded. If you're careless they'll take you. You

make one rash move when the cleaners are near...
then that's it – game's up."

I shifted across the creaky leather seat
toward Ben. Leaning in close, I could see the faint
stubble shading the lower half of his face. His eyes
flicked nervously from the wing-mirror to the lane
up ahead. "What are they?" I wanted his answer. I
had him cornered. I wouldn't give up until he told
me. I was so close to him now I could smell him. His
musky aftershave still lingered from when he'd
examined me on Ward 2 last night. "Tell me."

Ben turned to face me. A faint shadowy-
wave rippled over the blue in his eyes. "Demons.
They are demons without a body to dwell in."

CHAPTER THREE

I sat back in my seat, my eyes fell upon the satchel that I had taken from the chapel in the grounds of Cruor Pharma. Father Williams's journal was tucked inside. Max and I hadn't read it all. We'd skipped entries – desperate to find some answers about Cruor Pharma. Max had been anxious to know if there had been anything written in the journal about his missing brother, Robert. After hearing Ben's answer about the cleaners, I remembered the last entry that Father William had written. It had read:

I know now what evil lives amongst the walls of Cruor Pharma. I know what resides within Doctor Middleton. He is possessed. A demon has taken him.

Ben's answer wasn't really much of a surprise. Although I had believed the cleaners to be something else other than demons. They weren't the same as Ben, Doctor Middleton, and Doctor Wright. On the outside, Ben looked just like any other human being but the cleaners – they certainly couldn't be mistaken for humans.

"So, what's the difference between you and the cleaners?" I asked. "How come you look normal and they look like monsters?"

"The demon inside me is strong. I don't know much about him. I get little snippets of him when he's trying to control me. He hasn't been strong enough to take me over completely like the demon inside Doctor Middleton but he's been powerful enough to dwell in my body and keep it preserved for way too many years possible for a human to live. The cleaners are weaker. They don't seem to be able to dwell inside a human. I've seen several attempts of a cleaner entering a human body – taking it over – possessing it, but it never worked. The human body just couldn't cope with it dwelling inside. You've seen it yourself – Carly. Look what it did to her. It sends the human brain into meltdown – turns them insane. Doctor Middleton wants to find human bodies that can withstand his servants – not weak humans that turn into vicious evil monsters that can't be controlled."

"So that's why he does those fucked-up drug trials. He's searching for the right type of human body." I looked down at my hand and ran a finger over the lumps that clotted my vein. I prodded it gently – almost afraid to touch it – scared that it would push the VA20 around my veins quicker. "I guess the human body just isn't enough for the cleaners – is that why we've been fed VA20?"

Ben nodded his head. He pulled the van into a layby and switched the engine off. Taking my hand he said, "VA20 is dark matter taken from demons. Not just one but from six. I have no idea how it turned the other volunteers to crazy, killing monsters and not you. Your friends also seem to have taken it without any consequence. You are the first humans to survive this – the first ones who haven't gone insane. I don't know what it will do to you, but Doctor Middleton's idea was to take a human body and feed it with dark matter so it would be more compatible with a demon. I don't know if this drug will kill you but what I do know is that every demon will want you and Cruor Pharma is not the only place that has demons wandering about. They're out there – looking for a body and a demon knows a good catch when they see one. I think that's why I find the demon hard in me to control when I'm near you. It can sense there's something different about you – you excite the demon in me."

A small flash of black appeared in Ben's eyes then disappeared again. I pulled my hand away from his. I stared quietly out of the window. There was nothing to see except swirls of thick fog and hazy dark shapes of trees. It was silent. Even the birds hadn't come out. My mind slowly worked through everything that Ben had told me and then I remembered something he had mentioned back in the hospital.

"What about Doctor Langstone? You said that he might help me. Do you think he will?" I shifted round in my seat so I was facing Ben. I couldn't spend the rest of my life on the run – that was impossible. I had to find help from someone.

"Doctor Langstone didn't like the drug trials that Middleton and Wright were doing. He was quite happy to leave the cleaners as they were. He moved away after the first couple of drug trials went wrong," said Ben. "But, he has a demon in him as strong as Middleton and I don't know how he will react to you. You see, the problem is, a demon who has been quite happy living inside a human body might come across you and decide that you are a better body to dwell in, especially now that you have VA20 in you. You really need to stay well away from demons."

"Tell me about it," I said, glaring at Ben. "I can't stay like this. If there's a chance that Doctor Langstone might help me then I should take that risk."

"I think it's too big a gamble to take,

27

Kassidy. I think you should just keep moving from one place to the next and have as little contact with other people as possible," said Ben. "You don't want to end up like me – do you?"

"Of course I don't but I don't want to be running from demons for the rest of my life either," I snapped. I turned away from him. My eyes caught sight of something in the wing mirror – something dark coming out of the fog. I froze.

Ben must have noticed the sudden look of fear across my face. "What's wrong?" He leant over me and stared into the mirror. "Shit, it's the police. Climb into the back and keep down."

I didn't need persuading. I climbed over the back of the seat and pulled the black curtains shut. Crouching low, I steadied myself by placing my hands on the floor of the van. I immediately took them away when I felt something wet and slimy on them. Blood. I gagged. I'd forgotten that the back of the van was covered in it. I frantically wiped my hands over the back of Ben's seat. I'd seen and felt enough blood to last me a lifetime.

"Keep quiet," hissed Ben. "Inspector Cropper's coming over to the van."

I tried to steady my breathing – gulping down a mass of fear that was pushing its way up my throat – threatening to explode in a loud gasp. I felt sick. The fear of being caught and taken back to Cruor Pharma filled me with dread. What would happen if Ben's demon showed itself? Would it give me up? Hand me over to Inspector Cropper?

"Morning, Doctor Fletcher. What's this then – time out? I'm surprised you ain't driving up and down these country lanes in search of your missing volunteers."

"I have been, Inspector Cropper. Unfortunately, I haven't come up trumps yet. I pulled over to have a think about where they might be heading," said Ben. "What about you?" Had any sight of them yet?"

"Only from one of my constables who thinks he saw a blonde-haired girl climbing into a black van up on Strangers Hill."

There was a short pause. I held my breath. Was Inspector Cropper going to ask to search the back of the van? I turned my head to see if there was anything I could hide behind. As my eyes adjusted to the dark, all I could see was an empty space smeared in blood. My eyes fell upon something shiny where my knees rested on the floor. Picking it up between two fingers, I held it up. It was an I.D badge, the name printed on it was Nurse Jones. As I lifted it higher, I could see a clump of bright orange bloodied hair attached to a flap of skin hanging from the pin behind the badge. I wanted to throw it away, but instead, I calmly placed it back on the floor. I couldn't risk being heard. I screwed my eyes shut as I tried to rid myself of images of Wendy in the morgue and Nurse Jones being taken apart by the cleaners. The hideous pictures were snapped away as I heard Inspector Cropper begin to talk again. His voice was full of suspicion.

"Are you sure you ain't seen her, Doctor Fletcher? It's vital we get her back and the others. Can't have a bunch of murdering freaks on the loose. I don't want my police force coming under questions like I'm sure you don't want the reputation of Cruor Pharma to come under fire – I think you know what I mean."

"I understand perfectly well, thank you," said Ben. "I'm sure Doctor Middleton will pay you well for all the inconvenience this has caused. Now if you don't mind, Inspector, I would like to continue my search."

"Just remember, Doctor Fletcher, we need to be singing from the same hymn sheet. I'll scratch your back if you scratch mine – get me? You don't want to be crossing me – the shit I've got on you is enough to have you sent down for life."

"And the shit we've got on you is enough to

have your life wiped out, Inspector – don't go forgetting that," hissed Ben.

The sound of heavy boots on gravel crunched past the side of the van. I tiptoed to the back window and peered through the only clean spot. Inspector Cropper looked nothing more than a towering thug – a giant who could crush me in his large hands with one swipe. I watched as he stooped down to get back into his car. His bulbous eyes sent a shiver through me. Within minutes, the rumble of the police car slowly died away as it disappeared into the fog back the way it came.

The curtains separating the front of the van from the back were pulled open allowing some light to filter in. I turned to find Ben watching me.

"Thanks for hiding me," I said, taking a step nearer to him. I wanted to make sure that his eyes were still that crystal-blue before I got too close. I looked down at my bare feet. The soles were covered in blood as were my knees. I shrugged it off. What did some more blood matter when I was already covered in so much?

I climbed back over the seat and sat down. In the silence, I thought about what I'd heard between Ben and Inspector Cropper. I wondered how much the police knew about Cruor Pharma. Did they know it was run by demons? Or was it just that they knew about the unauthorised drug tests and what it did to the volunteers? Did they really think we were to blame for all those deaths at the hospital? Was that all they believed they were covering up? I glanced at Ben – what shit did Inspector Cropper have on him? My thoughts returned to the blood in the back of the van.

"Whose blood is that?" I pointed my finger behind me.

"I don't know," answered Ben. "It was already there when I took the van. I'm guessing the cleaners removed some of the volunteers from Ward 2."

He was very casual in the way he answered – like it was no big deal – like it was an everyday occurrence – the norm. Didn't he care that he was driving around in a van that had been involved in the cover-up of several murders? But then again, why would he? He had played a part in all this.

I looked back at the wing mirror. I wanted to make sure that no one else was creeping up on us.

"Do you think Inspector Cropper will come back?"

"Probably," Ben shrugged. He leant forward resting his elbows on the steering wheel and stared out into the foggy morning. "I wish I could leave."

"Why don't you?" I said, twisting my bad ankle around. It had loosened up a little.

"I tried before. But I always end up back in Cruor Pharma. It's like I wake up and find myself back in the hospital – like I never really did leave. But I know I did. I just don't remember going back. The demon inside wants me to stay. It won't ever let me go too far."

The radio suddenly switched on, filling the van with the sound of Oasis singing *The Importance of Being Idle.* I snapped my head around and looked at Ben. A faint swirly black mist lingered in his eyes.

"Ben… are you still with me?" I whispered, scared I would wake up the demon in him.

"I don't want to let you go…" a deep voice came from Ben. He shook his head and gripped the steering wheel. "I… I… I'm still here," he struggled to stay in control. "I have to let you go, Kassidy. If I don't, the chances are I will wake up back in Cruor Pharma and you will be in the hands of Doctor Middleton and I won't remember how the hell that happened. I'm gonna drop you off in Holly Tree." He turned the key in the ignition and pulled the van back out onto the lane. "I can't stay with you – I thought I could, but I can't. I'm nothing but trouble."

CHAPTER FOUR

The atmosphere in the van was changing. I could feel it. I didn't need to look at Ben to know that the demon was coming back. As the van lurched over the bumps in the lane, it seemed to grow dark. Things were moving by themselves. I gasped as Nurse Jones's I.D badge was thrown at the back of my head. The windows had misted up and I stared in horror at the words that appeared in the condensation.

"Go get your old man a bottle of whisky."

"Dad?" I mumbled. No sooner had the writing appeared, it vanished and another message appeared.

"You killed your mother, you killed me."

My body had gone rigid – numb to everything except the message on the window. I struggled to breathe. My ears flooded with the beat of my pounding heart. How did these demons know anything about my family? Which demon was it? The same one that had possessed Carly? Or was it the demon in Ben? Was it really my dad talking to me? I was so confused. I didn't know what to think. Ben's shouts suddenly snapped me out of my dumbstruck trance like I'd been slapped across the face.

"It's back. I don't know how long I can hold it off!" yelled Ben. He struggled to keep the van on the lane. The tyres screeched as they took a sharp bend to the left.

As I reached out to hold onto the dashboard, I was pulled back into my seat. It was like a pair of hands had snatched me – holding me down – rooting me to the spot.

"*Stop it, Ben. Stop it!*" I screamed. I tried to pull away from the grip but it held me tight. I could feel hands around my throat – the pressure increasing. I frantically reached out for the door handle. The locks went down, trapping me inside. The van filled with static from the radio. Whispery voices echoed from the speakers – calling my name.

"Kassidyyyy... Kassidyyyy."

The voices were all around me – whispering in my ear – breathing down my neck. I gulped down air as I tried to release the grip around my throat but there was nothing physical to grab onto. The van sped up.

"I'm gonna get you to Holly Tree – I am." Ben's voice was full of panic but determination. He pushed his foot down on the accelerator.

"Just let me out," I gasped, my throat was

tightening – my chest heaved in and out as the force around my neck continued to squeeze. My eyes caught sight of a large sign along the lane as the van thundered past. Half a mile to Holly Tree. I didn't care about the police. I didn't care about my bad ankle – fuck the pain – anything had to be better than this. I wanted the attack over with. "*Ben*… just let me go."

"I'm trying to fight him… *he's too strong!*" shouted Ben.

"*Get the fuck off of me*," I choked, scratching at my throat. No sooner had I spluttered the words out the pressure went – vanished. I gasped in air – slumped back against the seat – exhausted, but it wasn't over yet. My eyes widened as the windscreen was suddenly peppered in black fluid. It shot up like two fountains and slowly ran down the glass in long strands of goo, like blackcurrant jelly that hadn't set. "What is that?"

"Blood," murmured Ben. "It's coming from the screen wash."

The wipers switched on. The black goo smeared across the glass, leaving a wet trail of thick blood. Clots of flesh clung to the wipers as they moved back and forth. It almost seemed to wriggle as it flapped about over the windscreen. I couldn't believe what I was seeing. How was this happening? Where did the blood come from? There was so much of it. It hit the windscreen in a torrent of hailstones shooting up like an eruption of lava. The van was filled with the noise from the wipers frantically swishing over the bloodied glass. Even on full speed they struggled to keep the windscreen clear. I tried the door again. It was still locked.

"I can't see where I'm going!" shouted Ben, slamming his foot down on the brake.

I was flung from the seat. My arms shot forward, waiting for impact, but I was pulled back by Ben, grasped tightly in his arms.

"It's okay," he breathed. "I've got you. The blood's gone."

"Where did it go? How...?" I shook my head, staring at the windscreen, which was now clear. "How does that shit happen? Did you do it?" I looked up into his face. It was dark – covered in shadow like he had his own personal storm hanging over him. Behind his angry black eyes there was something else. A deep sadness seemed to hide in them. Flecks of blue floated amongst the rage that thundered in his eyes. A hurricane was brewing and the eye of the storm was trying to fight back.

"I can make anything happen." A deep,

sharp voice cut through the silence. "But I'm trying to stop myself. Ben doesn't want me to hurt you. He thinks you've been hurt enough."

I sat, still wrapped in Ben's arms. The demon was talking to me. I felt myself shudder. I didn't know how to respond to it. I didn't want to make it angry. I had to get out. But I didn't want to leave Ben. I knew there was good in him – but he was trapped and there was nothing I could do about it. I took a deep breath. "Why don't you leave Ben? Why do you stay in him?"

The voice cackled. "I like living in Ben. I can do whatever I want. My own body has rotted – fallen apart. It sits in its coffin, decaying. Why would I want to go back to that?"

"What about Ben? He wants his life – you've taken it from him," I snapped, trying to wriggle free from Ben's arms.

"Ben's life is long over. He'd be dead if it wasn't for me. I *give* him life. I could give you life, too. I could be your companion – *your constant*." Ben's grip tightened around me.

"I don't want you, I want Ben," I said, pushing my hands against his chest.

"You can't have him – not without me." Ben's hands released me and snatched at my hair pulling me toward him. The pain shot through me. I could feel my hair ripping from my scalp. I reached up, my fingers frantically trying to release the vice-like hold he had on me.

"Get off of me!" I knew it was pointless even asking but it was a natural instinct to say it. "You said Ben didn't want you to hurt me." I wanted to pull away but I couldn't. I found myself moving closer to him just to release the pain - my face was just inches from his.

"I want to hear you plead, Kassidy. Beg. Beg me to let you go." Ben's lips brushed over mine. His black eyes stared into me. He pulled on my hair – a glimmer of amusement in his eyes. "Beg me, Kassidy – it turns me on."

I pulled my left hand down into my pocket. My fingers searched out the rosary beads that I had taken from Father Williams's corpse. I found them – my hand curled around the beads and I snatched them out. I held up the rosary beads in front of Ben. "*Leave – me - alone*," I shouted. "I won't beg for you."

A low, guttural laugh came from deep inside of Ben. He yanked on my hair, lifting me half off the seat. "Rosary beads won't help you against me – I'm too strong."

I grabbed at his hands, the pain was too much. My eyes began to brim with tears of agony and the helplessness I felt at not being strong enough to fight him off. I wasn't going to beg this demon but I could plead for Ben – plead for him to fight this demon and come back.

"Ben, help me. *Please, Ben*, I need you. I can't do this by myself." My scalp felt like it was on fire – a searing heat eating through my head. I let go of Ben's hands and took hold of his face. Staring into his black eyes, I willed for that glimmer of blue to appear.

"Ben likes you but I like you more." The grip on my hair loosened. The evil black stare of his eyes seemed to weaken – fade. A look of sorrow filled his pupils as a ripple of blue flashed through them.

"Ben? Can you hear me? Please, I need you to let go of me," I whispered. "You need to wake up – don't let it take you."

"Kassidy?" Ben peered up at his hands. "Shit, what was I doing?" He let go of my hair and shook his head. "You need to get out." He took hold of the door handle and yanked it down. It was still locked. "Move back," he ordered, smashing his elbow against the window. The glass fell away in tiny pieces. "Climb out."

I snatched up the satchel and climbed over Ben's lap. "What about you? What are you going to do?" I asked as he lifted me through the window.

"It doesn't matter about me – don't concern yourself," he snapped. "Just get away from Holly Tree and keep moving. One of your friends – isn't a ..." He stopped mid-sentence and screwed his eyes shut.

"Isn't a *what*?" I asked, slipping through the window, my bare feet touching the ground.

"Next time I catch up with you, Kassidy, *you will* beg for me." Ben had gone again. I took a step back from the van – unsure of his comment. Was the demon really letting me go? He sat and starred at me, tapping his fingers slowly on the side of the van. His nails had gone black and were twisted out of shape. A thick plume of swirly smoke belted out from the exhaust mixing with the fog. I took another step back, like I was a chess piece moving away from the rook – waiting for his next move. I could feel myself tremble.

Run, Kassidy! that voice inside screamed at me. But I didn't want to turn my back on him – leave myself vulnerable. I shifted further away – my eyes never leaving Ben. Just a few more steps back and then I would feel safe in turning and running. As the fog swallowed up the van and I lost sight of Ben, I turned. I could still hear the tap-tap-tap of Ben's fingernails cutting through the fog. I had no idea of my bearings. I knew I was on the outskirts of Holly Tree but I didn't care. I ran.

CHAPTER FIVE

Fear made me run – made me forget the physical pain I felt with each movement of my body – each stride I took on my bad ankle. Fear pushed me further on. The tap-tap-tap of Ben's claws seemed to echo down the narrow winding streets of Holly Tree. I ran blindly through the fog – disorientated – scared that my escape would be stolen away from me. I was free but it didn't feel like that. Cruor Pharma's icy grip would never let go for too long. With each stride I took, I could feel the cold flutter of fingers snatching at my shoulders. Was it Ben? Was it the cleaners? Or was I just being paranoid? Who would blame me for feeling like that after everything I had been through? I was too scared to turn and look. The old buildings that lined the cobbled streets seemed to tower over me like they wanted to smother my escape – like they were a part of Cruor Pharma's trap. I pushed on. The place was empty. The streetlamps burned a gloomy orange through the fog making them appear to be glowing eyes watching me. I had to stop. I needed to catch my breath and work out where I was. I had no idea how far into the town I had got and how near I was to The Fallen Star. Would it be a mistake to stop? Would it be my downfall? *If you keep running into the unknown then you'll be in trouble,* that inner voice whispered to me. I felt myself slowing. My brain had got through the fright and was now trying to gather its strength and think straight. I ducked into a nearby doorway which offered me a little cover from anyone who might be wandering the streets looking for me. I bent over, my breathing heavy. The beat of my heart pounded away inside my head. I needed to calm myself down. My eyes were met with the sight of black veins running down the inside of my right leg. The toenails had become discoloured and my skin had taken on a greyish tint. I leant back against the wall. I had no time to stress about my veins, I could do that later, after I escaped from this place. I peered around the edge of the doorway. I needed to see some kind of a landmark that I would recognise, then I could work out which way I needed to go. My eyes slowly adjusted to my foggy surroundings and I could just make out a shop on the other side of the street. It was Doughy the Bakers. I had been buying cinnamon buns from there since I was little. Trying to picture the layout of the street without the fog, I knew I was on

Catchers Lane. If I followed it up to the end and turned into Trap Street, I would come across a narrow cycling path that would run alongside Stumble Brook. From there I would come out onto Corner Lane and The Fallen Star would be at the end of it. I could probably make it in ten minutes – quicker, maybe, if I ran. I glanced left then right down Catchers Lane. Was I alone out here? Was it safe for me to go? I couldn't really see very far through the fog, just dark shadowy shapes of buildings and the glowing eyes of the streetlamps. I listened. All seemed still. The residents of Holly Tree would be stirring soon and I didn't want to be wandering the streets when that happened. I needed to go now.

Slipping out from the doorway, I cautiously made my way down the lane keeping close to the shop fronts and under the canopies. I wanted to stay as hidden as possible. Although the fog was making it hard to see where I was going and worried the hell out of me as I couldn't see if anyone was about, it also worked in my favour too. I would be harder to be spotted by any prowling eyes that happened to look out of their windows. Ben's warning about not trusting the people of Holly Tree played on my mind. I turned onto Trap Street and remembered that the cycling path was just past Glugs' – the off-licence – a place I knew too well, thanks to my dad. As I went past the window full of bottles of wine and whisky, I caught sight of my reflection. What a mess. I really did look like I'd been to hell and back or spent the night in Glugs, emptying the entire stock down my throat. As I entered the narrow path, I could hear the gentle sound of sloshing water running over the stones in Stumble Brook. It was darker down here with no streetlamps and only a little light coming from one of the cottages. I looked up at the window. The curtains were still shut. I carried on down the path. Not too much further to go. I felt nervous. I was so near to my way of escape that all sorts of bad ideas started to flood my mind. What would I do if Jude, Max, and Raven had already gone? How would I know if they had left without me – I didn't even know what car Jude had? What would I do if the police were waiting there for me? What if Ben was awaiting my arrival? He knew I was heading for The Fallen Star. *Stop stressing, Kassidy – you won't know until you get there.* I tried to push all the negative thoughts away. I had to stay focused. I stopped. I had reached the end of the path and was now looking onto Corner Lane. There were a couple of shops on the other side that were still shut. As I peered through the fog to my left, my eyes flicked back to the upstairs windows above the shops. Was that a curtain twitching at the window? Was someone watching me? Had the town been informed that there were escaped volunteers on the run – murdering volunteers on the loose? I looked over my shoulder, back down the path the way I had come. Apart from the fog it was clear – no dark shadows. I stared back at the window, waiting for the curtain to twitch again. Nothing. I let out a sigh of relief and turned right onto Corner Lane. I had only gone a few steps when a car pulled in at the top of the lane, its headlights shone through the patchy fog. I felt my heart flutter as the car slowed down, almost to a crawl as it passed me. I tried not to stare – tried to act like I was just any-old person taking a walk through Holly Tree. At least it wasn't a van from Cruor Pharma, just a small white car. Could it be an unmarked police vehicle? I had no idea. I carried on walking. I wanted to break out into a run but that would just make me look suspicious. The urge to look back over my shoulder was too much. Had the car stopped or had it continued on down the lane? My heart stopped fluttering when I spotted the car turning off into another street. I carried on walking, a little faster this time. I could see the hanging sign for The

Fallen Star just up ahead but no sight of Jude, Max, or Raven. My eyes started searching the cars parked along the lane. There were five in all. Which one was Jude's? Did it even matter? Without Jude the car would be useless to me. I stood by the arched doorway to The Fallen Star. What should I do – wait? But for how long – they may never turn up and I didn't have time to spare. I wanted to be off these streets as soon as possible – away from the people of Holly Tree. If I didn't wait what were my other options? I thought of my friend, Hannah. The original plan was to get Jude's car and drive to the next town, The Mumbles, where Hannah lived. I couldn't walk there, it was way too far. I could catch a bus – but that was an option I didn't really want to take. It would mean waiting at the bus station and people seeing me. The train was out of the question – I would have to walk right past Holly Tree Police Station to catch one. It seemed that my only choice really, was the bus, but did I have enough money for a ticket? I only had a few coins which I had found in Father William's satchel. As I stood and thought through my options, a car turned in at the top of Corner Lane. I crouched down. The light on the top of the vehicle cut into the fog in waves of flashing blue. Shit. I crawled across the cobbled pavement toward one of the parked cars outside the bar, hoping that it would shield me from view of the police.

"Please go past, please don't stop," I whispered. I peered up at the car I was hiding behind and reached for the door handle. Locked. I could crawl along to the next car without being seen. I might just get lucky and find a car that hadn't been locked. On my hands and knees, I slowly moved along the path until I had reached the next car. I knew the police had stopped. The blue light continued to light up the lane. I heard a door open and two voices filled the silence. One was male, the other female.

"Inspector Cropper wants us to carry on our search in town. He thinks we're wasting our time up on Strangers Hill. He wants us to check all dark vans for that girl who was seen getting into one."

"Okay, Sarge," A female voice spoke. "Has Unit Two had any more sightings of the other three?"

"They were last seen running past the library about ten minutes ago. Unit Two lost sight of them. They could be anywhere in town but we've got the train station covered and Unit Three is heading over to the bus station. They won't be able to leave town so easy."

My heart picked up. I suddenly felt hopeful

that perhaps our plan to get Jude's car would still work. If my friends had last been seen outside the library about ten minutes ago, then they couldn't be too far from The Fallen Star. Maybe they were here already – waiting for the police to move on. I looked to my right. I was only two cars away from the top of Corner Lane. If I crawled on my hands and knees I could probably get round the corner and wait there, out of sight from the police. I started to move. It was hard work as I had to hold the satchel up so it wouldn't drag on the ground and make a noise. Trying to crawl low on only one hand was difficult. I only hoped that no one would look out of their window and spot me sneaking away from the police.

"We may as well move on, Sarge. There doesn't seem to be anyone around here," I heard the female officer say.

"Thank you," I breathed, but as I said it, I started to wobble. Not wanting the satchel to drop to the ground, I tumbled over to my left, knocking into a car parked along the side of the road. An alarm rang out – the car lights started to flash. Shit. I had set the car alarm off. I didn't have a moment to think. I jumped up. Knowing that I only had a few seconds head start before the police officers were on me, I ran.

"Oi." Their voices rang out behind me – their footsteps closing in on me. I reached the top of Corner Lane and in my blind panic to flee, I ran straight out into an oncoming car. The sound of brakes squealing cut through the cold, foggy morning. The car grinded to a halt just inches from me. Believing it to be another police car, I went to flee, but then I heard someone call my name.

"Kassidy, get in!" I stared at the driver's window. I couldn't believe it. Jude was sitting behind the wheel. The back passenger door flew open – Raven peered out – her eyes wide with fright.

"Stop right there – don't move," the female officer yelled. She was just feet away from the car – her sergeant, calling for back-up on his radio, stood a little way behind. Her eyes wandered down my legs and she took a step back – a look of revulsion stretched across her face – or was it fear?

There was no way I had any intention of handing myself over. I ran to the car and flung myself in. The wheels screeched as Jude slammed his foot down on the accelerator. Thick plumes of exhaust smoke swirled frantically in the morning gloom. Pulling my legs in, I reached for the door and pulled it shut. The car span around, almost knocking the police officer from off her feet. With the roar of the engine filling the car, we headed down Dodge Street, and away from the town of Holly Tree.

CHAPTER SIX

"Shouldn't we be heading down some of the quieter roads?" I yelled over Jude's shoulder. "The police are bound to have some kind of roadblock set up along here, it's the main street out of Holly Tree." I checked over my shoulder to see if we were being followed.

"Don't worry, I've got it covered. The police are too busy hanging out at the bus station." Jude grinned at me through the mirror. "They've got a unit over at the train station as well."

"Hey, Kassidy, it's good to see you made it down Strangers Hill." Max turned in his seat so he could see me. His green eyes looked worn but they still held that happy glimmer in them.

"It's so good to see you all too. I didn't know whether you had got away and if I should still go to The Fallen Star. I lost sight of you both back at Cruor Pharma by the fence. I thought I was gonna get crushed when the fence came down," I said, leaning back in the seat. I turned to look at Raven. She sat slumped with her legs curled up on the seat. Her greasy black hair hung over her eyes.

"Are we still going to your friend's house?"

she muttered. "I want to change these clothes and wash off all the evil that's tainted them."

"Yes, I think we should. I know Hannah will help us. But we can't stay there for too long," I said, remembering what Ben had told me. "I've got some stuff that I need to tell you all and it's not good."

"Fire away, Kassidy," Jude smiled, "I could listen to you all day long." He shifted the gear-stick down to third and turned the car onto a remote country lane. A large sign on a bent post read "Please come back and visit Holly Tree." I shuddered at the thought. I would never be able to go back to Holly Tree, and a part of me was glad to see the back of it, but I couldn't help but feel a little sad. All my childhood memories were there and even though most of them were full of sadness and loneliness, they were a part of me. My dad's grave was there. Would I ever be able to go back and talk to him? Maybe one day I could. Perhaps if I could get some answers about my dad then I'd be able to understand him – try and fix the emptiness that filled me – understand why he chose a bottle whisky over me every time. My fingers gently slipped over the photo that I had found of him at Cruor Pharma. It was the only picture I had of him now.

"Well, come on," hissed Raven. "What do you need to tell us? That taking part in drug trials can kill you?" She glared at me.

"I think we've already discovered that one, Raven," I muttered. "What I need to tell you is probably gonna sound crazy but hey, we've all seen plenty of crazy shit since yesterday, so here goes." I took a deep breath and told them everything that Ben had said and how he had gone from being Doctor Ben Fletcher to some psycho demon.

Max let out a deep sigh and ran his fingers through his hair. "So we've been injected with something called black matter from six different demons? And this is because Doctor Middleton wants human bodies to house his cleaners?"

"Yes. And they're not gonna stop hunting us until they catch us," I said. "I know it sounds mad but..."

"Too right it sounds mad," snapped Jude. "Demons? What the fuck is Doctor Fletcher taking? He's nothing but a fucked-up, crazy schizophrenic. What a load of..."

"It's true, Jude. I was there in the van with him. I didn't imagine blood pouring down the windscreen and I didn't imagine his eyes turning black and his nails twisting into long dark claws!" I shouted. "I know what I saw and you know what you saw at Cruor Pharma. You saw the cleaners. You can't sit there and tell me you think that they're human."

Jude sat and shook his head. "I think what happened at Cruor Pharma was a dodgy test that should never have been allowed and it went wrong. The doctors are bent and the police are bent and they cover up for each other. They don't want us back for *demon purposes*, they want us back because they don't want us exposing what they've been up to. Every one of those doctors is human – I don't believe in all this *paranormal shit*."

"Well after everything I've seen in Cruor Pharma, my brother's disappearance, and Father Williams's journal," Max's voice rose, "I'm thinking that what Kassidy has just told us is all true. Yeah, the police are as bent as hell but the doctors and the cleaners are something else – no way are they human."

I leant forward in my seat so I could see Jude's face, "*We* are probably not all human either anymore." I stuck my arm through the gap between Max and Jude. The black veins almost seemed to pulse under the skin like rippling waves in an oil spillage. "Stop pretending what they are – what we might be."

"So we're the devil's subjects now?" hissed

Raven. "I told you all. *Why* didn't you listen to me? Why did you stand and watch those demons hold me down and inject me with the *devil's curse*?" She threw her arms up and swung them about wildly like she was conducting a fast-paced symphony. *"We're gonna die, we're gonna rot in hell."*

"Shut up, Raven," snapped Jude. "I don't wanna hear that bullshit." He swung the car left and pushed his foot further down on the accelerator. "We're out now, we got away. Let's just chill – sort ourselves out at your mate's place and then... then we can take it from there."

I slumped back in my seat and stared out into the distance. I wanted to take hold of Jude and bang his head against a brick wall. Why couldn't he accept that everything that had happened to us was more than just bent doctors and police? He had seen so much, like the rest of us. The other volunteers on Ward 2. He had fought with them – ran from them. Hidden in a cupboard from the cleaners while they killed Nurse Jones. He had seen Carly possessed. Why couldn't he just open his eyes and face reality? I was too tired to argue with him, but whatever his problem was with the truth, he had better wake up and smell the coffee or he might just drag us all down and lead us into trouble.

We had been driving for twenty-five minutes in silence. Each of us preoccupied in our own thoughts. I had lost count of how many times I had looked over my shoulder to see if we were being followed. Jude had kept off the main carriageway to The Mumbles and had taken the quieter coastal route to avoid the police cameras. I looked out across the choppy waves and wondered how Hannah would react when we all bowled up to her flat looking like a bunch of bedraggled drug users. What would she think? I knew what she'd say. I could hear her clearly in my head talking in her snooty voice – *I told you it sounded too good to be true.* Well, she had been right and I hadn't listened. But regardless of her miss know-it- all ways and her snooty voice, I knew she would help us. Knowing Hannah, she would probably be drooling at the mouth when she clapped her eyes on Jude and Max. I glanced over at Raven. What would Hannah make of her? Even I didn't know what to think of Raven and I'd spent a night with her.

I snapped out of my thoughts as we turned onto the main road which led to the marina. We were only a few minutes away from Hannah's flat now and I glanced about – a nervous anticipation of what may lay ahead filled me. I felt relieved that we had reached Hannah – made it this far – but that feeling of dread lingered in the pit of my stomach. How long should we stay here? How much time did we have before the cleaners found us? Could they really find us here? I hadn't told Ben we were heading to Hannah's, it was only the four of us that knew of our plans so surly we would be safe.

"You said Christchurch, didn't you?" Jude asked, turning his head slightly so he could hear me. He had slowed the car down and put on the right-side indicator waiting for my response.

"Yes, Christchurch Road," I said, "Number four." I stared up at the block of flats which circled the marina. They each had their own balcony and were decorated with pot-plants and hanging baskets and had a view over the boats that moored here. *Lucky Hannah,* I thought as I pictured my own rented flat back in Holly Tree. It looked like a slum compared to this but I didn't even have that now – I was homeless.

Jude parked the car outside the first block of flats and turned the ignition off. "Well, we're here, shall we go in?" He turned in his seat so he was facing me.

I looked out through the window. The

marina was quiet. Just the gentle sound of water lapping at the boats and the distant cry of seagulls. It seemed void of all life, but after a closer inspection, I could see small spouts of smoke puffing out from some of the boats. I wound down the window. The smell of sea salt and frying bacon filled the car and made my stomach rumble. I felt a little relieved knowing that there were people about and that they were going about their usual business – cooking breakfast and not peering out at us from closed curtains like in Holly Tree.

"Come on," said Max. "If we're gonna go in then let's do it now while there's no one about." He opened his door and swung his legs out.

Taking a deep breath and snatching up the satchel, I said, "Okay, let's go." The cold air hit my bare legs and I couldn't wait to borrow some of Hannah's clothes so I could get out of the horrible blood-stained hospital gown and cover up the ugly veins that stretched under my skin. I shut the car door and headed for the first block of flats. A small gold plaque was fixed to the wall with numbers one to four in black writing. I pulled on the door and it swung open. Stepping inside, I found myself in a small hall painted in a light cream colour. There was a stairway and a lift and the door to flat number one.

"Let's take the lift," whispered Max, pressing the button to go up. He flicked his blonde hair from his eyes and gave me a reassuring smile. But behind that look I could see he was troubled – like he had the weight of the world on his shoulders. Poor Max. He was probably thinking about his brother, Robert, and whether he would ever see him again. I looked at Jude and wondered what was going on inside his head. Behind his cool, friendly manner I wondered what he really thought about everything that had happened to us. I didn't buy his explanation of Cruor Pharma and the doctors just being bent, and I didn't believe that he really did. Maybe it was just his way of dealing with it all? Blocking out reality so he didn't have to face it. And what about Raven? I stared at her from under my matted blonde hair. I didn't know anything about her. She hadn't once mentioned her family or why she had even volunteered to be a part of Cruor Pharma's drug trials. All I knew of her was that she was weird – obsessed with the devil, ghosts, and evil. But that wasn't really so weird anymore, not after a night in Cruor Pharma and a van ride with Ben. My heart almost stuttered when I thought of Ben. What was it about him that seemed to play on my heart-strings? I felt sorry for him. He wanted his life back. I believed him. I didn't think he was some kind of schizo like Jude thought. I had seen the demon in him – heard its voice – seen what it could do. Ben was trapped and if he couldn't do anything about it, what hope did I have of helping him? But there was something more than just sorrow I felt for him. I wanted him. There were emotions in me that made me feel desperate for him – a longing – a need to have him. But those feelings were wrong. I shouldn't be thinking like this. I felt bad for even fantasising such thoughts. Ben was bad. He was trouble. I almost felt like I was betraying the others – siding with the enemy. And that was wrong. Why couldn't I hate him – be fucking livid with him for what he had done to me – to my friends? I felt angry with myself. My stupid heart was ruling me and not my head.

A small bell sounded in the hall and the lift door slid open. I followed the others in. A sudden thought came to me – one that reassured me that maybe my feelings for Ben weren't my fault.

"Flat Four," Max whispered, pressing a button on a silver panel.

I nodded my head, too lost in my thoughts to speak. Maybe it wasn't my fault. Maybe I didn't have these feelings for Ben. Maybe they were for Ben's demon? It had pulled me in – hypnotized me – messed with my head. Maybe his demon had got under my skin?

CHAPTER SEVEN

The lift door opened. We stepped out into a small corridor. It was painted in the same cream colour as the hall downstairs and had a window overlooking the marina. I looked at the only door with a gold number four attached to it. I suddenly felt anxious – nervous. Not because I thought that Hannah would turn us away but because she was gonna see what I looked like. I almost felt ashamed – embarrassed that I had let myself get involved in something that Hannah had said was too good to be true – something that Hannah would never even think about doing. It was like having to go home and confess to your parents that you had been caught doing something terrible – the shame of it.

"Kassidy, are you gonna knock or shall I?" asked Jude, holding his arm up, knuckles curled tight ready to bang on Hannah's door. He looked at me with his flirty blue eyes, a small smile twitching at his lips.

I took a deep breath. "I'll do it. She won't want you hammering down her door," I said, stepping forward. I knocked gently. The others had crowded around behind me. I could feel Jude take hold of my hand, his fingers lightly stroking the top of my skin. I looked up at him. He winked and smiled at me. I pulled my hand gently away from his. It had been okay last night – a little flirting between us, before all the shit had happened, but now, I was in no mood to start all that again. Jude was hot – looks-wise but he wasn't for me. I stared back at Hannah's door. No reply. I knocked again, a little louder this time. If Hannah wasn't home, then where would we go?

The silence in the hall was suddenly interrupted by the noise of chains and a key turning in its lock.

"Who is it?" Hannah's voice asked from behind the door.

"It's me, Kassidy," I answered, letting out a sigh of relief that she was home.

"Kassidy? I thought you weren't coming round until tonight," she said, pulling open the door. Her eyes widened at the sight of us standing outside. "What on earth is going on? Who are these people, Kassidy?"

"Can you let us in, Hannah?" I asked. "I know we must look a right mess but I need your help – we all need your help."

"Of course, but..." Her voice trailed off when her eyes fell upon my right leg. "Oh, my god, what's happened to you? Kassidy... your leg – it's all... its... shit... that drug trial... what did they put in you?" She stepped to one side and let us in.

"Alright," smiled Jude as he strolled past her into the lounge. Hannah frowned as Max came forward

"Hi, I'm Max," he said, holding out his hand to her. "Thanks for letting us in."

Hannah went to shake his hand but pulled away quickly when her eyes fell upon the black veins protruding from under his skin. "Oh shit... it's on you too."

"Hey, it's okay, Hannah, it's not catching," I said, feeling like I had the Bubonic Plague.

"Well how would I know?" she said, screwing her nose up when Raven stepped in like there was a bad smell in the room. "Go through into the lounge." She flicked her hand like she was dismissing us and shut the front door. "Don't sit down on my sofas – I'll get some towels to drape over them first." She disappeared into another room then reappeared with a pile of towels, placing them over the cream-coloured sofas. "There you go," said Hannah, gracefully holding out her arms like she was displaying the crown jewels, "You can sit."

I sat down next to Max. *I Will Never Let You*

Down by Rita Ora played quietly from an iPod dock in the corner of the room. Raven plonked herself into a beanbag and Jude stood by the door leading out onto the balcony. He hooked his fingers under the venetian blind and peered out through the gap. Hannah stood nervously in the middle of the room, unsure what to make of us all.

"Okay. What's going on? What has that place done to you?" she asked, her eyes jumped from Raven to Jude to Max and then fell upon me.

"Hannah, we don't have a lot of time. We need to clean up, borrow some clothes, and I need some money. We're in loads of trouble and the police are after us," I started. "Not just the police but…"

"Hold on… just slow down, what kind of trouble?" asked Hannah. "Why is there dried blood on you?"

I looked down at my hands. Where was I going to start? "The drug trial at Cruor Pharma… it was bad… I mean… *really fucking bad*." I could feel myself begin to tremble. "Some of the volunteers turned crazy… like… like… zombies. I know that sounds mad, Hannah, but it happened. They tried to kill us… eat us… they could crawl up walls and even though their bodies had gone rotten and their organs were hanging out… they were still alive." I stopped to take a breath. Hannah just stood with her mouth open – dumbstruck. "The doctors injected us with a drug called VA20. They said it was to strengthen the immune system but it wasn't… it was just a big fucking lie."

"What was it then?" asked Hannah, looking at my legs again, her face full of revulsion.

I looked at the others. Max fidgeted. Raven just sat peering out from under her black strands of hair, and Jude nodded his head at me as if to prompt me on. I guessed they thought it should be me doing all the talking as Hannah was my friend. "This is the part that you're gonna find *really hard* to believe…" I let out a nervous giggle. "Hannah… the drug had black matter in it… six different types… from… demons." There, I'd said it. I'd told her. I stared up into her brown eyes, waiting for her response. Her eyes said it all.

"This isn't funny, Kassidy," she snapped. "You turn up here early in the morning looking like shit with some strangers who also look like shit and then tell me some horror story… I'm your best friend… why are you treating me like some bloody joke? Demons? Zombies? Black matter?" She placed her hands up to her head, running her fingers through the thick brown curls that sat on her shoulders.

I stood up. "I'm not treating you like a joke. This isn't some made-up story. It's true… it's *all true*. Please, Hannah… when have I ever lied to you?" I could feel my eyes welling up. If my best friend wouldn't believe me then who would?

"It's the truth," said Max, getting up and standing beside me. "I get why you don't want to believe it, I really do, but Kassidy is your best friend. Look at the state of her. Look at her legs, her neck." He looked at me. "Take the jacket off and show her your arm." Pulling on the sleeve of my jacket, it slipped off, falling to the carpet leaving me in nothing but the blood-stained hospital gown.

Hannah gasped and took a step back. My right arm had gone the same greyish colour as my leg. The fingernails had all turned a cloudy black and had grown in length into twisted points. The veins stuck out like burnt tree twigs under grey tissue-paper. Even I was shocked at how bad I looked. I bent down and scooped up the jacket quickly, sliding it back on. I didn't want everyone staring at me – *I* didn't want to stare at me either.

"We need your help," said Max. "But if you don't want us here then we'll leave."

Jude came away from the door. "We should have just gone to my place instead of wasting time

69

coming here. Let's just go."

"No. Wait. I'm sorry. Of course I will help you," whispered Hannah. "It's just… just hard to take in. Sorry, Kassidy." She placed her hand on my arm. "You should call the police. Those doctors need locking up." She turned and reached for her mobile.

"No! The police are in on it," I said, "They're out looking for us – trying to frame us for the murders of the other volunteers."

"And Fred Butler," said Max, unzipping the leather jacket he had taken from the locker room back at the hospital.

"Don't forget Nurse Jones," hissed Raven. "We're wanted for her death as well. We had to hide under a desk while those *evil-dead things* ripped her apart – I've felt her spirit – she's here with us now – haunting every step we take."

"Well, what can I do to help?" asked Hannah, taking a step away from Raven and nervously looking around her lounge as if in search of Nurse Jones's spirit.

"A shower would be good," smiled Jude, removing his shirt. "Something to eat and a drink. I don't mean tea or coffee either."

"You're not having alcohol," I said. "You have to drive, remember?"

"One ain't gonna hurt, it will wake me up," he grinned, eyes wandering over me. "Fancy joining me in the shower?"

I tutted and rolled my eyes. "Just hurry up in there, we all want to get clean."

"Yeah, be quick," spat Raven. "I don't want to be walking about any longer with dead people's blood and guts over me."

"Lead the way then, Hannah," smiled Jude, unbuttoning his trousers and ignoring Raven.

"It's just through that door," she pointed, her eyes taking in Jude's body as he brushed past her out of the room. "I'll sort you out some clothes, although I don't think I'll have any men's clothing to give you."

"No worries, Hannah," said Max, sitting back down on the sofa. "I'll be fine with these and a shower."

I left Max and Raven in the lounge and followed Hannah into her bedroom. It was painted in red and cream and had a large double bed placed under the window. Her dressing table was covered in bottles of perfumes and body lotions. She pulled open her wardrobe and started thumbing through her clothes.

"Where will you go when you leave here?" she asked, pulling out a pair of jeans.

71

"I'm not sure yet," I answered, sitting down on the bed. "I have to keep moving. If I stay in one place for too long then they will find me."

"But you need to get help, Kassidy. Whatever it is they injected you with, you need to get it out of you. What about St. Martin's hospital? There must be something they can do," said Hannah, taking a pair of black leggings from out of a chest of drawers.

"If I walk into a hospital looking like this then I'll get locked up. They will call the police and then I'll get taken back to Cruor Pharma. I can't take that risk," I whispered. "I never want to see another hospital in my life."

"When will I see you again?" Hannah came and sat down beside me. "If you're gonna be on the run then... will I see you again?"

"I don't know. There's a doctor that may be able to help me but I don't know if he will want to." I looked at Hannah, her sad brown eyes stared back at me. "I wish I could stay here with you. I wish I didn't have to leave."

"I wish you had just come to me and asked for money instead of volunteering your body for two thousand pounds. I would have given it to you – I would give you anything. You've been my best friend since we were little kids. You're like a sister to me. My dad thinks of you like his own daughter. Why did you do it?" Hannah asked, taking hold of my hand.

"Pride, I guess. I didn't want to come over and beg for money. I'd already lost my job, which made me feel useless. Dad left me with nothing but debt, so to ask you for money was just another embarrassment I couldn't face…" I trailed off and chewed my bottom lip. "But now I'm in a worse situation than ever – I've messed up again."

"You have to get help," said Hannah. "That black stuff in your veins might kill you – god only knows what it's doing to you. Do you feel ill?"

"No, just tired and hungry – battered and bruised," I whispered, looking down at my ankle. It didn't hurt as much as it had. I lightly touched the bite mark on my neck where Carly's teeth had bitten through. It seemed to have dried up but still felt sore, and I could still feel the sting from Howard's bite on my stomach. What I really needed was to sleep. My head felt fuzzy and my eyes stung. If only I could just lie down on Hannah's soft bed for a while and shut my eyes but I daren't. I would never get back up again and that was time I couldn't afford.

"Here, take these." Hannah handed me a pile of clothes. "There's something for you and that strange girl to wear but I don't have anything for the other two unless they want to wear women's clothes."

I looked at the clothing and pulled out the black leggings and a roll-neck top. That would be good to hide the bite mark on my neck. That left a pair of jeans and a pink floral blouse for Raven. "I'm gonna need some boots and gloves – I have to keep my hands covered," I said, staring at the ugly veins that twisted under the skin like a jagged pathway.

Hannah stood up and opened a drawer. She rummaged around until she found some gloves and then she went back to her wardrobe and pulled out a pair of long black boots. "You can have this as well," she said, throwing a leather jacket onto the bed.

"Thanks, Hannah," I whispered, placing the pile of clothes down beside me. I pushed my hands into the pockets of my jacket, the tips of my fingers lightly brushing over the iPod which I had taken from Ward 1. I looked around Hannah's bedroom and spotted another iPod dock on her bedside table. "Hannah, can I use your dock to charge this up?" I held up the iPod.

"Sure you can," she smiled, "is it yours?"

"No, I found it on one of the wards at Cruor

Pharma. I'm hoping it might have some evidence against the doctors that I could use if I ever get caught or if I ever pluck up the courage to walk into a police station and tell them what happened." I placed it into the dock and pressed the button. Would it even work? The screen lit up, an image of a run-down battery appeared, indicating it was as flat as a pancake but at least it was showing signs of working. Hopefully if I let it charge up while I had my shower I might be able to see what was on it – if there was anything on it? It seemed strange where I had found it. Up the end of Ward 1 away from the bagged up items of passports and mobiles, almost like one of the past volunteers had smuggled it onto the ward – and why would they do that? To film in secret was what I was hoping for.

"Maybe if you get out of this county, you could try another area's police force. One that has nothing to do with this county," suggested Hannah, placing some fresh underwear onto the pile of clothes she had given me. "They can't all be bent."

"No, but I don't know if Holly Tree police force will issue a warrant for our arrest. They may alert all the other police forces around the border of this county. If I'm gonna go into a police station then it will have to be one that is far away from here, and it's not something I'm planning on doing until I get myself back to normal – until I've seen this other doctor. I don't want to give the police any ideas that I'm infected with something that has turned me into some crazy, killing loony. That will just give them reason to have me locked up in some secure mental hospital." My mind wandered back to Sylvia Green. I didn't want to end up like her.

"How do you know this other doctor will help you – if he can even help you?" asked Hannah. "Do you even know where he lives – works?"

"He works at Cruor Pharma's sister company in Derbyshire. It can't be too hard to find," I said, standing up.

"Is that really wise?" frowned Hannah. "If he's a part of the same company that did this to you then surely you'll just be walking into a trap."

"I have to give it a try," I sighed. "There is no other option." Reaching into my pocket, I pulled out the photo of my dad. "Hannah, I need to ask you something."

"What is it?" she asked, stepping toward me.

I handed her the photo of my dad. "Do you ever remember hearing anything about my dad working for Cruor Pharma – anything at all that your parents might have mentioned?"

Hannah stared at the photo. "Shit, I never remember ever seeing your dad work but ..." she turned the photo over in her hands. "This was taken when we were young, how would we ever remember?"

"What about your mum and dad, did they ever talk about my dad – ever mention my mum?" I asked, hoping that I would get something from Hannah, anything, even just a little snippet about my parents.

"Your mum? Why ask about her? You've never spoken much about her in all the time we've known each other, why now?" Hannah handed the photo back to me.

I shrugged and shook my head slowly. "I don't know... I just heard some weird things about her at Cruor Pharma – strange things..."

"Like what?" Hannah took hold of my hand. She could see I was struggling to tell her – see I was getting upset.

I took a deep breath and swallowed down the lump that was forming in my throat. "Like... she loathed me – wanted me dead." I chewed on my bottom lip and blinked back the tears that had gathered threatening to spill like a broken dam. "My dad hit the bottle to drown me out... he was never proud of me... I was a drain on his life. They're both dead because of me... I... I..." My face cracked. My lips trembled and the dam finally broke. The flood from my eyes streamed down my face and pooled at the corners of my mouth. I pulled my hand away from Hannah's and covered my weeping eyes. I felt so weak. Not just physically but weak as in feeble. "Everything's such a mess... I don't know what to think anymore... it's like my brain has been thrown into a blender with all these different emotions and problems and it's been turned on – full blast. I can't think straight... what did I do to make them hate me?"

"Now you listen to me, Kassidy," Hannah shouted, "I don't know who's been telling you this dreadful nonsense, but it's all shit. You never made your dad hit the bottle, that was his choice. And as for your mum – she died when you were two – how could a two-year-old be blamed for her death? Whoever told you this rubbish needs locking up."

"But there must be some truth in it... how else did they know about my dad being a drunk? They got that right, so what's to say that they're not right about my mum?" I wiped the tears away from my face and stared at Hannah.

She lowered her eyes and looked at the floor. "All I know is that you have been the greatest friend I could have ever had. You are kind, you're funny, and you've always been there for me. You don't have a bad bone in your body – now tell me, how can someone like that be responsible for the deaths of their parents?"

I looked at Hannah. How could it be my fault? She was right – I was only two, barely responsible for myself, let alone two parents. But still... that didn't explain how Carly, or whatever was in her, had known such private things about my life if there was no truth in it.

"As for my parents – I don't remember them speaking about your mum – ever. They did talk about your dad, though, but nothing to do with him working for Cruor Pharma," Hannah said. "They used to get really angry about the way he looked after you – or the lack of it. I think you spent more nights sleeping at ours than in your own bed."

That was true. Hannah's parents had looked after me way more than my dad had. If I hadn't had them, my life could have been a lot worse.

There was a gentle tap on the bedroom door. "Shower's free, Kassidy, if you want to jump in?" Max called. "I'll go after you."

I opened the door. Max stood with his blonde hair draped down the sides of his face. His leather jacket hung open revealing a toned set of muscles covered by a pale-grey skin. A thick black vein ran across his chest from the right side and had started to snake its way up his neck. Another faint black vein could be seen running up from his navel. I had no idea what the rest of my body looked like underneath the hospital gown but I guess I was soon to find out as I headed for the bathroom.

CHAPTER EIGHT

I dropped the hospital gown to the floor and stood in front of Hannah's full-length mirror with my eyes shut tight. I was almost too afraid to look – too afraid to see the truth. I didn't want to know how far VA20 had spread. I knew it would be bad but so far I had been able to ignore the rest of my body – only being able to see my hands and legs. I could just step into the shower and not look at myself – not face the horrible truth, but what was the point? This black-shit wasn't going anywhere soon so why bother to snub it? *Just look, Kassidy. Get it over with and face it. You're not the only one here who looks like this,* my inner voice said. Still, it didn't make it any easier to confront.

"Okay, let's do this," I whispered, opening my eyes. I stepped back. A gasp lodged itself in my throat. I tried to swallow but my throat was clogged up – my heartbeat like a drum-roll. The right side of my body looked like I had a circuit board in me – a series of black wires connected to each other – pulsing, like electricity was running through them. If I stepped back further from the mirror they could almost be mistaken for some kind of weird tattoos. I turned around and looked over my shoulder. Again, the right side of my body was plagued with VA20 twisting under the flesh on my back. Add that to the greyish skin and the bruises that I had gained from my night at Cruor Pharma – and not forgetting the two bite-marks – I looked fucked. Frowning at myself in the mirror, I stood and stared at the ugly mess and lost myself for a good ten minutes in a daze. That voice in my head woke me from my hazy thoughts. *Time – don't forget the time – you have to keep moving.* I opened the shower door and stepped in, turning the dial on the hot water, I let it splash over me. Steam rose from off my skin and clouded up the shower cubicle. A bottle of shower gel hung from a hook and I squeezed a large blob of orange-smelling gel into my hands. Rubbing them together to form a lather I cleaned away the blood, dirt, and as Raven called it – *the evil* that tainted our skin. It felt good to be rid of everyone's blood – to be rid of death. I reached for the bottle of shampoo and scrubbed away at my scalp. It hurt from where I'd had the hair ripped out by the cleaners and where Ben's demon had pulled on it, but I didn't care – I just wanted to be clean. Lifting my face toward the water, I let the shampoo run down over my forehead, into my closed eyes and down my cheeks. I waited for the water to run clear and then slowly opened one eye at a time. As I blinked away the watery haze, the shower cubicle almost seemed to shudder, like someone had knocked into it. I blinked again – unsure of what I had seen. Had I imagined it? Had the water in my eyes played tricks on me? I stood still. I listened. All I could hear was the sound of running water spraying onto me and hitting the floor in splatters. I turned a full 360 degrees slowly – always listening. It was like I was back out on Strangers Hill trying to find my way through the fog. The cubicle was full of steam and I reached out to rub it away from the door of the shower. I didn't want to do it. The last time I had felt like this was when I had almost pulled open the curtain that had separated Ward 2 into two halves. *"The grass isn't always greener on the other side,"* came to mind as I remembered the sight that had greeted me up on that hospital ward. Pulling my hand away from the door, I held it to my chest. I stood still. Should I wipe away the condensation? What wonderful sights were awaiting me on the other side of the door? Hopefully just an empty bathroom and the realisation that sleep deprivation really isn't good for you. I took a deep breath. My fingers touched the steamed-up door and cleared a small circle, just big enough for my eye to peek through. I didn't want to make a huge gap in the condensation. If there was anything on the other side then it wouldn't be able to see me peering through. I leant forward and pressed my eye up to the small circle I had cleared. Nothing. The bathroom was empty. I let out a huge sigh. Turning back to face the water, I rinsed off the remaining suds from my body. A loud thud to my right made me jump. The whole cubicle shook. Pressing my back up against the side of the glass, away from where something had hit the cubicle, I stood rigid.

"I didn't imagine that," I shuddered. "Who's there? What do you want?" I reached up and turned the water off – my ears straining to hear anything that seemed out of the ordinary. "If that's you, Jude, I'm gonna kick your arse." No reply. "This isn't funny, you know, after everything that's happened to us, you shouldn't be trying to scare me." Still no response. I looked down at myself, and as if suddenly realising that I was completely naked for the first time, I pulled my arm up across my chest and my left hand down between my legs. If that was Jude out there I wasn't gonna give him the pleasure of seeing me naked. In fact, I didn't want anyone to see me like this. I shivered. Drops of water dripped from the ends of my hair and dribbled down over my skin in cold trickles. What should I do? I turned slowly toward the door and peered out through the small hole. It had started to mist over again. My finger squeaked over the glass as I cleared some of it away. The room seemed empty. There was no movement – no sound, just the drip-drip-drip from the shower-head. I didn't know what was worse. Not seeing anything but knowing that you weren't alone or coming face to face with whatever had banged into the cubicle.

"Hannah," I yelled out. Maybe if someone heard me, they might come in and whatever was in the room with me might go? "*Max, Raven, Jude.*" Why wouldn't they answer me? I chewed on my bottom lip. As I leant forward again and peeked out through the hole in the condensation, something dark flittered past. I stepped back. I wasn't alone. Shit. I franticly looked about me. What could I use to defend myself? There was nothing. A couple of shampoo bottles and a sponge wasn't gonna cut it. The water suddenly shot out from the shower-head – full blast. I spun around. I reached up to turn it off but the dial had stuck. Another bang on the side of the cubicle sent me slipping to the floor – the water continued to pour out. I stared open-mouthed as the shower-head started to twist and come loose. "*Max, help me.*" I tried to get up but

the soapy suds left me with no grip. I slipped back
down landing on my arse. Using my feet and hands
I pushed myself back against the shower door – my
eyes never leaving the shower-head as it continued
to twist itself free from the silver-coiled hose.
Squeak – squeak – it dropped to the floor between
my feet. The water jetted out from the hose as it
hung from the rail. I reached up behind me and
pulled on the door. It wouldn't budge. My fingers
slipped on the handle. I tried again. Twisting myself
around, up on my knees, I made another grab for
the handle. The glass shuddered as I put all my
weight against it. It was stuck. My wrists were
grabbed. Something held them tight. My arms
were pulled away from the door. I lost my balance
and tumbled back, hitting my head on the floor. I
stared up at the hose as it came toward me. The
strength of the water hitting my stomach with such
force it sprayed up into my face. I couldn't get up.
Something held me down. I wriggled about trying
to loosen the tight hold it had on me – water
sloshed over my face – gurgled in my ears. I could
feel hands on me – icy-cold fingers on my flesh.
They grabbed at my face and slipped into my
mouth – stretching open my jaw – wide. I tried to
bite down – tried to close my mouth but the grip
was like a vice – a tight clamp that wouldn't budge.

I snatched up at the hose as it came toward me. The wet coils slipped through my hands as my wrists were snatched away and held down above my head. The silver hose shoved into my mouth – hitting the back of my throat. I gagged as the water rushed down. I threw my head from side to side – kicked my feet out – smashed at the glass door with my left foot – hit out at the side panel with my right. I lifted my hips from off the shower tray so I could use as much force against the door. I tried to pull my arms away but they were held firm above my head. Hot water poured down my throat and cascaded out of my mouth like a fountain. I swallowed and swallowed. There was too much – too much. My lungs were filling up. I was drowning.

"Kassidy, are you all right in there?" Jude's voice sounded through the gurgling water. The door to the bathroom rattled. "*Kassidy*?"

The icy fingers lifted its hold on me. I sat up. The shower door was open. The silver hose was hanging above me with its shiny shower-head still fixed in place. I pulled myself up – stunned. What the hell had just happened? I didn't imagine it. I touched my throat and swallowed. It felt fine.

"*Kassidy*, can you hear me, what's going on in there?" Jude shouted.

"I… I'm… all right," I answered, stepping

from out the shower – stunned. I stood in the middle of the room and shivered. Wrapping my arms around my stomach, I turned slowly. The room was empty. There was no sign of the struggle that had just happened. Everything was in place. I looked down at my wrists. Not a mark was left on them from where they'd been held down. I shivered again – my teeth chattering. Snatching up a blue, fluffy towel, I wrapped it around me and took one last look back at the shower cubicle. Everything was where it should be. There was no trace of the attack I had endured. As I went to turn toward the bathroom door, my eye caught sight of something in the bottom of the shower tray. Some kind of grey, gloopy liquid had been squeezed over the floor to form the words, *"Get out, Kassidy – leave."*

CHAPTER NINE

I opened the bathroom door. Jude stood outside. He was back in his shirt and trousers but smelled clean and flesh. His black hair had a shimmer to it and his skin looked smooth and soft.

"What was all the banging about in there? You look like you've seen a ghost," he asked, his eyes checking me from head to toe as I stood in just the bath towel.

I pulled it up higher over my chest and said, "Look in the shower – on the floor, there's a message."

I waited just outside the door. I didn't want to go back in there. Jude came out, a look of confusion over his face, "I can't see anything, Kassidy. Are you sure you didn't imagine it?"

"No, I didn't imagine it. There was something in there with me – I nearly drowned." I could feel myself getting upset. "It held me down and shoved the fucking hose down my throat."

"What's going on?" Max walked out from the lounge, a clean towel in his hands.

"Kassidy thinks there was someone in the shower with her," sighed Jude. "I think you just need a good sleep – we all do."

"Yes, I do need to sleep but I know what I saw – what I felt. I'm telling you, something was in there – something has followed us from that *fucked-up hospital*," I snapped, hugging the towel tighter around me.

"What did it look like?" asked Max, nervously eyeing the opened door to the bathroom.

"I... I... don't know. I didn't see it, exactly," I said, knowing that I now sounded like I had an overactive imagination. "I felt it. It grabbed my wrists and nearly killed me."

"Do you think it was the cleaners?" asked Max, still peering into the bathroom.

"No, it wasn't them. They're different. It felt like there was just one but it had loads of hands," I said, looking at Jude and then back at Max. "It was able to hold me down by my wrists and hold my mouth open at the same time. Whatever it was, it wanted to kill me."

"You said it left you a message on the shower tray," said Jude. "What did it say?"

"It told me to get out – to leave," I whispered, looking back at the bathroom.

"Well that sounds a good idea to me," said Jude, running his hands through his hair. "Don't take too long in the shower, Max. I think we should go as soon as possible." Jude turned away and walked back into the lounge.

"Maybe I should just skip the shower," whispered Max, sticking his head slowly into the bathroom. "If we're in a rush to go, I don't want to hold everyone up."

"Have your shower," I said. "But don't lock the door – just in case. What about Raven? Has she showered yet?"

"She went in before you," said Max. "She fell asleep about ten minutes ago." He stepped into the bathroom cautiously and closed the door.

I walked into Hannah's bedroom. The clothes she had found for me were laid out on the bed. Walking past them, I headed for the window. Peeling back the curtain, I peered out. The view looked over the seafront and the main road into The Mumbles. There was very little traffic about, just the odd person taking a morning stroll along the seafront. Everything looked quite normal, yet it still didn't do much for the uneasy feeling I had inside me. The attack in the shower had left me shaken. Was this what life was going to be like now for me? Living on the edge – looking over my shoulder every couple of seconds? It seemed that the whole world was after me and my friends. Police – cleaners – doctors and whatever that was in the shower. I shuddered and wrapped my arms tight about me.

After dressing, I zipped up the pair of boots that Hannah had left out for me. Sitting at her dressing table, I gave my hair a quick brush and borrowed some of Hannah's make-up. At least I looked a lot better. I would be able to walk about in public without anyone thinking I'd been out on the town all night pissed and shooting-up shit with the local drug addicts. I sat in silence and stared at myself in the mirror.

The bedroom door swung open and Max came stumbling through, clutching a towel about his waist, clothes screwed up in a ball under his arm.

"Sorry," he said, "I thought you were finished in here." He turned to leave.

"It's okay, I'm done," I said, standing up. "How was the shower? Did you see anything?"

"Nothing. Just a nice, hot shower," he said, drips of water running down over his shoulder.

My eyes fell upon his chest. "I'm not the only one who looks like they have a circuit board in them."

He looked down at his body and nodded his head, "I've seen better days I think." He half-smiled and looked up at me. "It's weird, don't you think?

How can we have this shit in us but none of us have had any real effect from it? Why haven't we ended up like the other volunteers? How are we still standing and yet the others turned crazy?" He dropped his clothes onto the bed and flicked his wet, blonde hair from out of his face.

"I have no answers." I shrugged, "Only questions like you, Max. We have to get to Doctor Langstone's. I know it's a long shot but if anyone can help us, it's him."

He raised one eyebrow and sighed, "We could be walking into another nightmare. He's another demon, what's to say he won't take us – keep us for himself? We could end up just like Carly – end up dead."

"All I know is that I don't want to end up in the hands of Doctor Middleton, the cleaners, or the police – I think we can safely say that we're dead if they get their hands on us. Doctor Langstone is our only hope now. I know it's risky but I don't see any other way out of this mess."

Max sat down on the edge of Hannah's bed. He picked up a small towel and started to dry his hair. "I'll go to Doctor Langstone, but first, I need to find that Bishop. The one Father William sent my brother to. I need to know if he's still alive and where he is," said Max, staring at me with his green eyes. "I haven't gone through this nightmare for nothing. My brother is the only reason I signed up to be a volunteer, so I can't walk away from that – not until I know the truth about Robert."

I sat down beside him and pulled on the gloves that Hannah had found for me. "I told you I would help you last night with finding out what happened to your brother. I will go with you to the Bishop's, I promise." I took his hand in mine and gently squeezed. I knew how he felt. He needed answers just like I needed answers about my parents. We both had an emptiness that needed to be filled. Bad or good, we had to know one way or another.

Max squeezed my hand back and smiled at me. "Thanks, Kassidy. You know Jude won't be too happy with our plan. He's dead-set on us going to his place."

"I know, but we can't just hang out partying all day and night with him. If what Doctor Fletcher says is true, then we can't hang out anywhere for too long. Jude needs to open his eyes and accept the truth or he'll end up dead – and take us down with him." I stood up. "I'll let you get dressed and go and see if Hannah can look on the internet and find out where this Bishop lives." As I went to walk away, a sudden thought came to mind. "You know, we might be safe at the Bishop's. It's a holy place. I don't know a lot about demons but I'm sure church is the last place they would hang out in. Remember what Father Williams wrote in his journal? He called the chapel his sanctuary. He said they couldn't follow him in there. I think we may have just found ourselves somewhere we can rest safely for a while."

"That's if the Bishop don't mind," said Max. "He might not want to give up his home to help a bunch of people infected with demon shit."

I left the bedroom. Surely the Bishop would let us stay. He was a man of god. They were meant to help people in their time of need. As my head raced with thoughts of the Bishop, my heart jumped with the sudden notion that a Bishop could perform an exorcism. Would that get rid of the dark matter that was in us, or did we have to be possessed for an exorcism to work? I wasn't sure. All I knew was that going to the Bishop's would help us one way or another. If he couldn't perform an exorcism on us at least we would be in a place of safety – away from the cleaners and demons.

CHAPTER TEN

I walked into the lounge. *Take me to church*, by Hozier played gently from the iPod dock. Jude sat on the edge of the sofa – remote control in hand – flicking through the news channels, while he sipped from a bottle of Bacardi and Coke.

"What are you doing?" I asked him, my hands on hips.

"Just checking the news channel – making sure Middleton and Cropper haven't put something out there to the media about us. I haven't seen anything yet, so I guess the world ain't looking for us."

"That wasn't what I meant," I tutted. "Why are you drinking? It's still the morning and you have to drive."

"It's just one for the road – to wake me up," smiled Jude. "Chill, Kassidy, I'm not gonna drive us into a river or a building. I can handle my drink. I can handle anything." Jude looked me up and down. "You look good but the towel and wet body-look suited you better." His blue eyes shimmered as he took a swig of Bacardi.

I turned away, my eyes fell on Raven. She was curled up on the beanbag, stretching her arms and yawning. She wore the clothes that Hannah had found and her greasy black hair looked fluffier now that she'd had a shower. She had obviously helped herself to Hannah's make-up as her eyes were now stencilled with thick, black eyeliner and her thin lips coloured black.

"Why do I have to wear this shitty rosebud blouse?" Raven snarled, her eyes checking out the clothes I was wearing. "Why can't I wear what you've got on?"

"This wouldn't fit you," I said. "You're taller than me – it would look like a tank-top on you."

"I look like I'm off to *freaking* Sunday school," she hissed. "And look at these *stupid shoes* – they're pink with a bow on top." Raven stood up. Her scrawny legs looked even thinner now that she was out of the porter's trousers she had taken from the locker room.

"If you don't like them, then wear the porter's clothes," I snapped, feeling irritated by her ungrateful behaviour.

"I'm not wearing *dead people's* clothes," she scowled. "Their spirits follow you – haunt your every step."

I couldn't bear any more of her weird talk. "Then shut up and wear what Hannah has kindly given you."

I headed into the kitchen to find Hannah filling a small picnic hamper with food from the cupboards. She turned to face me.

"I haven't got much in the way of food to give you all. I haven't been shopping this week yet," she said, placing a pot of potato salad and a small box with chicken vol au vents into the hamper. "I've filled two flasks with tea and there's a bottle of milk and some sugar." She placed a pile of napkins and some forks into the hamper.

"Thanks, Hannah," I smiled, taking it from her. "Can you do me a favour? Could you look on the internet and find out where the local Bishop lives?"

"Okay," she said, a look of confusion on her face. "Why?"

"It's a long story. I don't have time to tell you," I said. "We really need to get out of here. The longer we stay, the longer we put you at risk. If we get found here, then you'll get caught up in this mess and I don't want that to happen."

"Follow me," said Hannah. "My laptop is in the lounge."

I sat beside her on the sofa. The screen lit up as Hannah started to search.

"What are you looking for?" asked Jude, turning away from the T.V.

The address for the local Bishop," I answered, my eyes never leaving the screen.

"It's a bit late to go praying now, don't you think?" said Jude. "The damage is done. No holy man is gonna help us. Look what happened to that other priest back at the chapel. He's fucking dead."

Hannah looked up at me. "Are you sure you want me to find this address? Is there nowhere else you can go?"

"My place. We can go to mine. It's safe and miles away from here," pushed Jude.

"I'm not going to yours," I argued. "If we go to the Bishop's, then we can rest up there for a while and Max can find out about his brother."

"He ain't ever gonna find out about his brother," said Jude, standing up and leaning over Hannah so he could see the screen. "He's probably dead."

"We don't know that yet," I said. "And keep your voice down. I'm sure those kind of comments aren't going to help Max."

"I just think," started Jude, "that we would be better off...."

"I've found it," smiled Hannah, cutting over Jude's voice. "He lives at Dusk Fall Retreat, Squire Village, Rane. St. George's church comes under the same address."

"Never heard of Rane before," I said, more to myself than Jude and Hannah. "Is there a map?"

"We don't need one," said Jude. "I know where Rane is. It's about an hour drive from here."

"Good," I smiled, relieved that we could reach it easily enough. "So are you coming with us?" I stared at Jude, unsure that he would want to, seeing that he so desperately wanted to go to his place.

"Of course I'm coming with you," said Jude. "We're in this together, aren't we? As much as it pains me to go on all these little detours, I know we are safer – stronger if we stay together."

"I want to go to the Bishop's," mumbled Raven, crossing her arms over her chest, trying to hide as much of the floral blouse as she could. "I want to know what happened to Max's brother – he might still be there."

"Have you found it?" Max walked into the lounge. His blonde hair was dry now and tied behind his head in a short ponytail. One loose strand dangled down the side of his face and he tucked it behind his ear. His leather jacket creaked with each step he took.

"Got it." I smiled, knowing that Max would be relieved, being one step nearer to finding out more about his brother. I could tell by the hopeful look on his face that he was glad.

"I guess we're ready to leave then," I said, suddenly feeling sad. I looked at Hannah. Would I ever see her again? I wished I could stay here with her or take her with us but I knew that neither were an option. If there was one person in this room I could trust with my life, it would be Hannah. I felt secure with her. She had been my one and only constant friend, and as I looked at the faces of Jude, Max, and Raven – and remembered the half-comment that Ben had started to say back at the van – they were no more than strangers to me. We had been thrown together in a nightmare and now I had to leave with them and trust in them. But did they really have my back? When push came to shove would they reach out and save me or save themselves?

CHAPTER ELEVEN

We stood in the hall by the front door. Raven leant against the wall, yawning, staring out quietly at us as we made sure that we had everything we needed.

I had emptied out the pockets of the jacket I had taken from the morgue and placed the photo of my dad and Sylvia Green's passport into Father Williams's satchel. The rosary beads I put on. The cross sat hidden under my top. After what had happened in the shower, I wanted the rosary beads close to me. How much they would protect me – I wasn't sure – but anything would do for now, at least until I got to the Bishop's.

"Ready?" asked Jude, taking the hamper from Hannah. "Are we going on a picnic?" He looked at the hamper with a bemused look on his face. "Where's the picnic blanket – you know, so we can pull over on our travels and sit by a nice lake and catch some sun?"

"There's no need for that sarcastic tone with me," said Hannah. "Some people like to dine in style. Greasy spoon cafes aren't for everyone you know."

"We're on the run," smiled Jude. "Dining in

102

style is the last thing on any of our minds."

"Well now you can be on the run in style," she answered, turning to face me. "Do you have everything you need, Kassidy?"

"Hang on," I said, slipping past Max and heading into Hannah's bedroom. I didn't want to leave behind the iPod that had been charging in the dock. As soon as we were in the car and leaving The Mumbles I would turn it on and see if anything had been filmed at Cruor Pharma. As I went to take it from the dock I realised that it had been switched off from the wall – the plug pulled out.

"Shit," I cursed. Why had someone turned it off, and who? Hannah wouldn't have done it but why would any of the others? They knew I had taken it from Ward 1 to see if there was any evidence we could use against Cruor Pharma. It made no sense. We were all running from the hospital, the doctors, and the cleaners so why do this? Should I go out into the hall and confront everyone – see who looked guilty? No. I would keep quiet and see if any of them waited for a reaction as I joined them back in the hall. *"One of your friends – you can't trust."* Ben's unfinished comment played through my mind. Maybe it was just paranoia that had me doubting my friends. Maybe the demon in Ben had been playing with me. But it had seemed that Ben had tried to warn me and then something had stopped him – midsentence. It was the demon that liked to play games – not Ben. So therefore, shouldn't I believe Ben's warning? That uneasy feeling I had felt a while ago was creeping back up on me. I didn't want to believe that Jude, Max, or Raven couldn't be trusted. We had all been through the same horrors – all been fooled into volunteering for the drug trial, so Ben's mistrust made no sense. Not unless he had found out something about one of them or had met one of them before? But where? As far as I could tell, Ben seemed to be pretty much kept up at Cruor Pharma. He didn't get to spend his time hanging out in Holly Tree and chatting with the residents, so where would he have met one of my friends before? I looked down at the iPod and turned it on. The battery life was near non-existent. I would be lucky to get two minutes out of it before it shut down again. Turning it off, I placed the iPod into the satchel. I really didn't know what to think about my friends and I didn't have time to stand here and analyse everything I had seen and heard. I would go back out into the hall and not mention the iPod and see if either of them happened to mention it. Turning my back on the iPod dock, I left the bedroom.

"Got everything?" asked Max. "We don't want to leave anything behind." He stared at me, those happy green eyes calm and gentle as always.

"Yep, I'm ready to go," I said, turning my attention to Raven – trying to read her face. She just looked as miserable and grumpy as she had since the moment I had first seen her in the reception at Cruor Pharma. I turned my attention to Jude who just stood and winked at me with his flirty smile. Nothing out of the ordinary across his face. That uneasy feeling felt too close for comfort. Those doubts I had had about trusting the others wouldn't go away. But neither of them had acted suspicious. No one had mentioned the iPod to me.

I looked at Hannah. All those times I had spent sleeping over at her parents' house because my dad had been too pissed to look after me and I had been too scared to go home seemed trivial now. Never had I wished so much that I could stay with her. But I knew that was out of the question. I had to put my trust and faith into Jude, Max, and Raven now. I was in this mess with them and I had to step out of my comfort zone and face reality, no matter how frightening it was – no matter whether I trusted them or not. I had to get away – keep moving, and staying with my friends was the only way I was going to keep one step ahead of everything and everyone that was after me.

"Take this," whispered Hannah, placing some money into my hand. "It's not going to last for long but it should keep you all going until you reach this doctor's place."

I looked at my hand and could see five twenty pound notes. "Thanks, Hannah." I placed the money into my pocket and zipped it up. She held out her hand and gave me a slip of paper. "What's this?"

"I wrote the Bishop's address down for you and on the other side is my dad's number and address if you need his help – you know, about your dad," she whispered quietly leaning into my ear. "Promise you'll ring when you get to the Bishop's. I won't be able to relax until I know you've got there safely."

"I can't," I said, suddenly remembering that my mobile phone had been taken from me under Doctor Middleton's orders. "My phone is still at Cruor Pharma. I had to hand it over shortly after we texted each other yesterday."

"There wasn't anything mentioned about this place, was there?" Jude suddenly spoke up. "I wouldn't put it past those freaks to go through your phone and check any messages – you know, to make sure that you hadn't told anyone about volunteering at Cruor Pharma."

I felt the colour drain from my face. Hannah had turned pale as we both looked at each other and remembered what we had sent in the text messages.

I chewed my bottom lip as I recalled the message that Hannah had sent me with her new address on it.

"Shit, you sent me your address," I whispered. I turned to look at the others. "Do you think they will check my phone?"

"Of course they will," hissed Raven. "They didn't think twice about going round to Nurse Jones's house and wiping her son off the face of the earth. You've led us all to our *deaths* – those demons are gonna get us now, and even if they don't, they'll come round here and torture the information about where we're going from *her*." Raven glared at me, her eyes narrowed to slits as she turned to face Hannah.

"What should we do?" I could feel the panic rising up in me.

"We need to leave now," said Max, his hand gripped the door handle. "Hannah will have to come with us."

"Go on the run you mean?" Hannah looked shocked at the suggestion. "I've never been on the run before – I don't know if I should?"

"None of us have been on the run before," said Jude. "You don't need a diploma or master's degree to do it. I'm sure you'll pick it up quick enough."

"Well how long will it take?" asked Hannah. "I do have a job, you know. When will I get back?"

"Hannah, if you don't come with us then you may end up dead. Anyone who might know anything about Cruor Pharma gets cleaned away," I said.

"And that's not a nice soak in a bubble bath," said Jude, raising one eyebrow at Hannah.

"The dead will come and kill you," hissed Raven. "They'll take you apart, bit by bit, or infect you like they infected us."

"I'll get my stuff and meet you down in the carpark," said Hannah, snatching her car keys and heading for the bedroom. She didn't need any more persuading after Raven's input.

"Hurry up," Jude called after her. He shoved Raven in the back toward the front door, his arms outstretched like he was herding a cow out into a field. "Shift Raven, you need to move faster than that."

We piled out into the cream coloured hallway. Max went to the small window and checked outside. "It seems okay out there, but then, would the cleaners turn up in a car? I doubt it somehow – they just appear out of nowhere."

"Take the stairs," I said. "The lift takes too long." As if something had been listening to me, the lift doors suddenly opened. The silence was broken by its sharp ping.

We stood and looked at each other, then back at the lift.

"I'm not going in there," hissed Raven, backing away toward the stairs.

"Don't tell me, let me guess," said Jude, "the lift's haunted?" He raised his eyes at Raven and then held his hand out for me to take. "Come on, we'll take the stairs."

We jumped two to three steps at a time. Third floor – second floor, our footsteps echoing up and down the stairwell. As we reached the ground floor, Max slowed up and turned around to face us.

"Let's just go out nice and calm," he said. "We don't want to draw any unwanted attention to us."

I looked back up the stairwell, hoping that I might be able to hear Hannah on her way, but it was silent.

Max held the door open and I stepped out into the morning. The smell of sea air and bacon still lingered. An old man walking his dog strolled past, he nodded his head and carried on by. We reached the car. Pulling open the boot, Jude threw the picnic hamper in and climbed into the driver's seat. I looked up at Hannah's flat.

"Come on, come on," I whispered, too on edge to sit in the car. I checked over my shoulder, looked up at the windows to the flats, and then toward the moored boats. Chewing on my bottom lip, I leant into the car and looked at Jude, "Do you know which way to go from here?"

He turned the key in the ignition and the car fired up. "I'll take the back roads. I know where to go."

"Which one is Hannah's car?" asked Max, sitting in the front passenger seat and looking at the four parked cars outside the block of flats where Hannah lived.

"The red one," I answered, opening the side door and placing the satchel on the backseat. Raven was already curled up – eyes shut tight. How could anyone fall asleep in moments like this?

"Kassidy, *Kassidy*." I turned and looked up at Hannah's flat. She was out on the balcony, waving her arms at me. "I'm coming now!" she shouted.

"Hurry," I called up at her. As I turned to

110

look away, something caught my eye. Hannah had climbed up onto the balcony rails and was now wobbling to and fro – her arms stretched out wide like she was balancing on a tightrope.

I gasped. "What the fuck, Hannah – *Hanna*h – *what are you doing – get down.*"

"I'm coming, Kassidy – wait for *meeeee!*" She bent her legs at the knees and jumped.

The world seemed to stop. It was like the only thing that existed was me watching in horror as Hannah fell – all my senses fixed on her body as she plunged like a rock. Hannah's voice screaming *meeeee*, filled my ears and cut through the morning silence.

"*Nooooo, no, Hannah!*" I screamed, the words slipped out before I could move. The sickening thud and crunch of Hannah's body as it smashed onto the roof of her car broke her haunting scream and woke me out of my frozen stupor. The roof of her car almost seemed to swallow her up from the impact as her head hit first – neck snapping to the side.

I ran. Jude's and Max's screams were nothing more than garbled sounds behind me as blood pumped through my body – heart threatening to burst from within me. I reached the car. Hannah's bloodied face peered out from under her crumpled body. Her skin hung like flaps of silky, peeled off wallpaper – shards of metal pierced her flesh. Her eyes were open but there was no movement.

"Hannah," I rasped. "Hannah!" I climbed up onto the bonnet – stretched my arm out and touched the side of her face.

"I'm coming, Kassidy," Hannah's eyes blinked – her body twitched like she was receiving electric shocks.

I fell back and tumbled from the car. How was she still alive? Slowly, I pulled myself up, gripping the side of the car. My hands trembled. I struggled to breathe. Did she really talk or was I just in shock – my mind unable to function?

"I'm coming – I'm coming – I'm coming." Hannah laughed a low guttural chuckle. Her pupils rolled to the back of her head leaving just the whites like two boiled eggs. She continued to twitch – her flesh still hooked and twisted on the metal. "Better run, Kassidy – I'm coming – Doshia is coming."

A hand fell on my shoulder and I spun around expecting to see the cleaners. It was Max. A look of shock stretched across his face. He stared at Hannah and tried to pull me away.

"We have to go *now*, Kassidy, come on." His

eyes never left the sight of Hannah's broken body.

"But Hannah... she's still alive... we can't..." I began, but Jude cut over me.

"She's not alive, that's not Hannah," said Jude, trying to turn me away.

"*Then how the fuck is she still talking!*?" I screamed, tears in my eyes. I shoved Jude away from me and swung out at Max as he tried to take hold of me. "*Get the fuck off of me... she's my friend*... my best friend." I turned back toward Hannah.

"Doshia knows *you*," Hannah spat. "You thought I'd gone, but I've been with you all along."

There was a cracking sound as Hannah tried to get free her head from the mangled up roof. Her neck snapped as the bones grinded against each other. The skin on her face stretched and tore like elastic.

"Right, that's enough," shouted Jude. "We're going." He snatched my wrist and dragged me toward his car. "Max, take her arm and help me."

I dug my heels in and struggled to stay rooted to the spot. What the fuck was happening? I'd escaped that kind of shit back at the hospital. This was my best friend – this was meant to be reality – normal life – but it seemed that wherever I went – the evil came too. I turned my head – one last look at Hannah. She lay slumped on the car, her body still now.

"*Come on!*" I heard Raven shout. She sat half in half out of the car, a look of horror in her eyes.

The distant sound of sirens floated across the marina, caught up amongst the cries of seagulls. I stumbled forward, almost losing my balance. Max and Jude held me up.

"Shove her in," I heard Jude say as he ran around to the driver's side and climbed in.

"Come on, Kassidy, we have to get away from here," said Max, forcing me into the car. "The police are coming."

I slumped back against the seat and watched the marina disappear as Jude pulled away.

I'm coming, I'm coming. Hannah's voice floated in my ears.

I shut my eyes to the vision of my best friend falling to her death – a sight that would never leave me – not ever.

CHAPTER TWELVE

I was flung from my seat as Jude slammed the brakes on, my face hitting the back of the seat where Max sat, my legs bent up and wedged into the foot well. Levering myself up by pulling on the chair, I sat back in my seat and peered out through the windscreen. A police van had just turned into the road up ahead and was driving toward us.

"Take a right," said Max. "Just drive nice and calm. Hopefully they'll go straight to the marina and by the time they've realised we've gone we'll be far away."

"Maybe," said Jude, "but for all we know my car might be down on their system to pull over. I'm pretty sure that when we left Holly Tree in a rush this morning, those two police officers would have taken down my registration plate."

Jude turned right onto a small residential street with a newsagents on the corner. Raven and I peered out of the back window and held our breath. If the police van carried on past then we would be okay – for now. But if it turned in behind us then we were in trouble.

"There it goes," shouted Raven. "It's not following us."

I watched as the police van sailed past the top of the street – a small victory but not enough to pull me out of the dark I now felt I was trapped in. I covered my face with my hands and closed my eyes. A replay of Hannah falling from the balcony started up and then repeated itself again and again. But did she fall? Had she been pushed? My brain tried to scramble together all the possibilities that could have caused Hannah's death. She wasn't pushed – she didn't fall. No one forced her to climb onto the balcony railings. No one told her to jump like a diver from a diving board. She just did it. She jumped like it was nothing.

"Your friend's dead because of that text message."

I looked at Raven. She stared at me with her dark eyes – her face angry.

"What?" I snapped. How dare she blame a text message on the death of my friend? "A text message made Hannah jump from a balcony, did it?"

"Those demon-cleaners must have been told to come here after they checked you're mobile. *It's your fault they're onto us*," she hissed. "You should have never suggested coming here. You may as well have stuck a knife in Hannah's back and been done with it."

"*Why don't you shut the fuck up!*" I
screamed, grabbing Raven by the collar of her
blouse and slamming her head into the back of the
seat. "That wasn't the cleaners' doing. It was
something else. Something called Doshia."

"*Hey – hey!*" shouted Max, turning in his
seat. "There's no point in fighting. It won't bring
Hannah back, Kassidy. I don't know what the hell
happened back there but it wasn't your fault." He
turned his attention to Raven. "And *you* need to
keep *this - zipped*." He pointed to his lips and
pretended to zip them shut. Max stretched out his
arm and pulled gently on my shoulder. "Let go of
Raven. No good will come of it."

"I don't know about that," Jude chipped in.
"Might give us some peace and quiet if someone
knocked her out."

I stared into Raven's pale face. Her dark
eyes glared at me. She gritted her teeth like she
was trying to stop herself from saying anything
more. She pulled on my wrist, her hand covered in
black veins – five cloudy misshapen nails dug into
my flesh. I slowly released my grip on her and sat
back. Hannah's falling body started to play in front
of my eyes again like an old projected film – hazy
and distorted. It flickered on-off-on-off, like each
scene had a glitch – a fault. I didn't want to see it

anymore but the image wouldn't go away.

"She had a demon in her," I said aloud, more to myself than to the others. "Doshia. Hannah said that Doshia was coming."

"Whatever that was in Hannah, it seemed to know us," said Max, looking in his mirror at me.

"Knew one of us," I corrected him, my eyes wandering from Jude to Raven and Max. "It was under the impression that whoever it knew, believed that it was gone, but it hadn't."

"How many demons did Doctor Fletcher say there were?" mumbled Raven, peering out at me from under her hair.

"Six," I whispered. "But that doesn't include all the others that are on the loose, wandering around the country looking for a body to possess. There must be six at Cruor Pharma, and then you have the cleaners. I don't know how many there are of them."

"So is this Doshia, one of the six?" said Jude, looking at Max. "I'm lost. All this demon stuff is crazy." He shook his head and stared out through the windscreen, taking a left onto the road which led out from The Mumbles.

"Maybe, I don't know," said Max. "But I'm hoping that when we get to the Bishop's we might find out some more about these demons, especially if my brother's there."

I looked down at my hands. I felt numb – emotionless. I wanted to cry. I had just watched my best friend fall to her death, yet the tears wouldn't come. They had dried up like an arid desert – my tear ducts in the middle of a drought. I was trapped in a deadened state – my feelings dulled and muted. I stared out through the window and watched the world go by.

CHAPTER THIRTEEN

We had left The Mumbles and were now travelling down the old B125, a single carriageway that weaved through the countryside. The road was pretty much empty. Every so often, we would pass through a small village, or by a farm in the middle of nowhere, but mainly just fields and trees. The sky had darkened over, grey-black clouds loomed above us, threatening a storm.

"We're gonna have to stop at the next service station," said Jude, cutting into the silence. "I've got less than a quarter of a tank of petrol – not enough to get us to Rane."

"You sure it won't be enough?" asked Max. "I don't fancy having to stop. What if someone recognises us?"

"I don't want to stop either but I don't want to run out of petrol – not here in the middle of nowhere," said Jude, checking his mirrors.

"Will there even be a service station out here?" mumbled Raven, shifting in her seat. "I haven't seen anything for miles."

"There's bound to be one soon," answered Jude. "These old roads used to be the main way of getting about the country until they built the motorways – they would have had to have petrol stations. And as for us getting recognised, Max, I don't think the police have issued any public warning about us. If they had, the roads would be teeming with police cars by now. I don't think Inspector Cropper wants any other police force to know about us and neither does Doctor Middleton. If they can get us back quietly then that's what they'll do. They ain't gonna risk drawing attention to what they've been up to, no way."

"I guess Hannah's death will be blamed on us," I whispered, staring out at an empty field.

"I think what will happen if we get caught by another police force – one that doesn't come under Inspector Cropper's area, we'll be framed for all those deaths – which means, we'll be handed back to Inspector Cropper as the deaths have happened on his patch," said Jude. "Which then leaves him free to hand us back to Middleton. Of course that's *not* how they want to get us back. We could say all sorts of things about Cruor Pharma and Cropper – enough to get people talking and digging around and Middleton – and the police have too much to hide, too much to lose. So if they can get us back without letting the public or other police forces knowing about us, the better for them. That's why we haven't seen a single police car since we left The Mumbles."

"Keep us hidden away like some *dirty little secret* you mean?" spat Raven, looking at her long twisted nails. "*I hate them, I hate them all.*"

"We all hate them, Raven," said Max, turning in his seat to look at her. "But hate isn't gonna help you, me, Jude, or Kassidy."

"What is then?" hissed Raven. "How do we beat them? We can't stay at this Bishop's place forever."

Ignoring Raven, I looked at Max and said, "Even if we did talk – you know – to other police forces about what had happened at Cruor Pharma, then we risk getting locked away and classed as insane like Sylvia Green. I don't see any good coming out of us harping on about Cruor Pharma. Just one mention of demons and volunteers climbing along walls and eating each other is enough for us to get sent down for life – they'll throw away the key."

"That's why we can't get caught," said Jude, his blue eyes staring at me through the mirror.

"But what is the answer?" I said, feeling frustrated. "I don't see an end to all this – do you?"

"We stay on the run, or we go to this Doctor Langstone in the hope that he can remove this black-matter-shit and then we stay low and hope

122

that Middleton and the cleaners give up," shrugged Max. "If what Doctor Fletcher says is true about our bodies being used for the cleaners to dwell in then they won't want us anymore if we can get rid of the VA20."

"They will," said Jude. "They'll just catch us and inject us again with the same stuff – now they know that you three can take VA20 – they ain't ever gonna let you go, they'll probably try it on me again or just kill me."

"Well I guess we've had it then," I snapped, "we may as well just turn around and invite the cleaners in. Why fight it?"

The car fell silent again. I turned and looked out of the back window. There must be a way. There has to be something we can do. I hadn't even considered the possibility of being re-injected. That put a spanner in the works of my plan to visit Doctor Langstone. But still, it seemed the only option available to us. Maybe if the black matter was removed then the cleaners would no longer be able to trace us? Was that how they worked? Did they sense us because of the VA20 inside our veins? Is that how they tracked us? If so, then maybe Max was right. We get it removed then stay low for as long as it takes. It was a chance – our only chance, unless we could come up with another idea – another plan.

The silence was broken with the sound of the indicator ticking on-off-on-off. I turned back in my seat as the car pulled into a small petrol station. There was only one other car at the pump. A middle-aged man stood filling up his red Jeep. His brown spiky hair looked like he had a hedgehog stuck on his head.

"Are you sure we should stop here?" mumbled Raven, sliding down in her seat. "We don't know for definite if our faces haven't been splashed all over the media."

"We need the petrol," said Jude, turning the engine off. "There might not be another chance to fill up the car."

"Well I'm not getting out," Raven said, folding her arms across her chest.

"I'll fill up, you go and pay, Kassidy," said Jude, getting out of the car. "I'll just put enough in to fill the tank a little. We need to be careful with the money – make it last."

"Why don't you come with me, Raven?" I said. I was feeling a little guilty about attacking her earlier in the car. I was still annoyed with what she had said but I hadn't been thinking straight and maybe Raven had been the same – we had just both witnessed another death – a death that should never have happened. Hannah hadn't deserved to die. She had helped us and it was because of her help that she was now dead. "Well? You could check the papers – see if there's anything in there about us? Maybe there's an article about our escape from Cruor Pharma?"

I could see Raven thinking about my suggestion. She took hold of the door handle then let go and slumped back into her seat. "I'm not getting out looking like *this*," she grumbled, staring down at her flowery-blouse. "I look stupid. It's all right for you with your nice black leather jacket."

"Here, take it," I said, pulling the jacket off and handing it to her. "But look after it – it was one of Hannah's favourites. I'll wait outside for you while you put it on."

I stood beside the car and waited while Jude filled it up. There was a cool breeze now and the clouds had got darker. I looked out across the forecourt at the empty fields. Apart from the low rumble of the petrol pump and the squawking of crows flapping about over the fields, the place was silent.

"Hey, I'm sorry about Hannah," I heard Jude say. "I know I can't do anything to bring her back but I'm here if you need a shoulder – a hug – or just someone to talk to."

I stared into Jude's eyes. He seemed genuine. Not his usual playful manner. I nodded my head at him. I wasn't ready to talk about Hannah – not yet. Not just because I found it too upsetting, but because I knew I needed to keep a straight head on my shoulders – needed to keep several steps ahead of everything and everyone that was after me. If I became an emotional wreck then I'd be no good to anyone, let alone myself. My eyes wandered from Jude's stare to the man with the red Jeep. He was leaning up against the petrol pump still filling his car, but his dark grey eyes were fixed on my face. I looked away, uncomfortable by his stare. That's all I needed right now – some weird perv. I flicked my hair so it hung over my face allowing me to peer at the man without him realising I was looking at him. I felt myself shudder as the man hadn't looked away. His eyes gazed right at me – unblinking, like there was nothing else in the world to look at – like he was hypnotized.

"Are you done?" I asked Jude, just wanting to pay and get away from the dissecting eyes of the weird man.

"Twenty quid," answered Jude, replacing the petrol cap. "That should be enough to get us to Rane."

"Come on, Raven," I said as she got out of

the car. She seemed happier now she was wearing the leather jacket. We turned away and headed for the small run-down shop on the forecourt. Taking the money from my pocket, I pushed open the door and stepped inside. The shop was cold and had two aisles that ran down the centre, filled with nothing much but the usual essentials. Bread, butter, tins of beans and tomatoes and cardboard boxes of eggs which looked like they had come from a local farm. It smelt musty and looked as though it needed a serious make-over. Raven headed for the newspaper stand. An old man sat behind a wooden counter wrapped in a blanket and wearing gloves. I walked toward him but kept my eyes on the forecourt through the grimy window. The weird man had finished filling up his red Jeep and was now heading for the shop. I didn't like him. The way he stared at me gave me the creeps. I reached the counter and looked over my shoulder as I heard the door to the shop open. Turning back to the old man I could feel myself tense. I didn't like having my back to some weirdo but then I didn't want to face him either – didn't want to engage his exploring eyes.

"Just petrol," I whispered to the old man, handing him a twenty pound note. I looked over at Raven. She was crouched down, flicking through the pages of a tatty-looking paper. I shivered. I felt the presence of the man bearing down on me. He was so close I could feel his breath on my neck – smell his sweetly-sick aroma. Who was he? One of Cropper's team? No, he couldn't be. We had arrived after him.

"Come on, Raven, let's go." I turned to leave, my head down avoiding his probing stare. He stepped to the right and blocked my exit. I moved but he barred my path again.

"I just want to talk," hushed the weirdo, his grey eyes bulged from their sockets and lingered on my chest. "Such a pretty thing you are. Why don't we find somewhere quiet where we can get to know each other?"

I looked at Raven. She stood, frozen to the spot. Her eyes wide with fear. I looked out at the forecourt. Jude and Max were sitting in the car – unaware of this freak bothering me in here. I swallowed hard and took a deep breath, "No thanks, I'm not interested." I tried to push past him. He stretched out his arm and brushed his fingers over my lips. He sighed like he was getting turned on and leant forward and sniffed me.

"You're divine," he hushed. "I bet you taste good, too." He pushed me against the counter and leant his body against mine. His face was covered in pock-marks and his breath smelt like soured milk. "Your body's empty, let me fill you." He smiled – his breathing heavy – faster.

I heard the old man behind the counter stand up. "Not in here," he croaked. "I don't want no trouble."

"*Get the fuck away from me!*" I screamed, reaching for one of the tins that were stacked on the shelf. I curled my hand around the cold tin and brought it down hard on his skull. Raven flinched and took a step back. I shoved him hard in the chest and the man lost his balance, tumbling to the floor. I clambered over him. His fingers curled tight around my ankle. He wouldn't let go. I could feel myself wobble. If I didn't get him off of me then I would end up on the floor with him. "*Let go.*" I tried to shake him off. The man looked up at me and grinned. Suddenly, a shower of tins fell – hitting him right in his pock-marked face. I looked up. Raven's arms were full of tins. She hurled them at the man like she was playing Dodgeball.

"Stop – stop." The man let go of my ankle and shielded his face against the onslaught of tins.

"Let's get out of here!" shouted Raven. She ran to the door and pulled it open.

Snatching a box of eggs, I flung them at the old man behind the counter, "*That's for doing nothing*," I spat, and headed for the door.

"Start the car!" I shouted at Jude, as I ran across the forecourt with Raven. Max could see the panic in our eyes and got out.

"What's happened? What's going on?" he asked, coming toward me.

"That man in there…." I breathed. "He touched me… he…"

Max looked over my shoulder, "The guy with spiky hair?"

"Yes, he grabbed me… wouldn't let me go." I tried to calm my breathing.

"I just want to talk to her."

I froze at the sound of his voice. He had left the shop and was now standing behind me. How did he have the nerve – the guts to continue his sick, fucked up assault in front of a group of people – my friends? I slowly turned to face him. His eyes ate me up as they roamed from my head down to my toes. His nose was bleeding – the blood gushed down over his top lip and dripped off his chin. He shifted his gaze to Max in one quick movement – drawn to him like a magnet. "You could come with me – if *she's* not interested." He sniffed the air like an animal hunting its prey.

"What the fuck…?" Max looked revolted. "Back off you sick fuck!"

"Get in your Jeep and *piss off now!*"
shouted Jude. He had got out of the car and was
now walking toward the man, his face full of anger.
"*Go - get the hell outta here.*" Jude jabbed his
finger at the man.

"There's no need to be so greedy, you
know," said the man, his eyes roamed from Raven,
to me, and then back to Max. "There's enough to
go around. I don't mind sharing." He licked his lips
like he was about to tuck into his dinner and
rubbed his groin.

"Get in the car, everyone," ordered Jude,
his eyes still firmly on the man. Raven didn't need
any prompting. She climbed in and yanked the
door shut – the sound of the lock thudded.

"We're leaving now," said Jude, still staring
at the freak. "And if I see you following us – I'll fuck
you up real bad."

The man stepped away – his hands held up
like he was surrendering. "Can't blame me for
trying," he grinned, blood still dripping from his
chin. He looked around Jude, his eyes lingered over
Max and then back on me like he was having one
last taste to savour.

I climbed into the back of the car and
locked it. Looking at Raven, I said, "Thanks for
helping me in there, I couldn't get him off of me –

he was too strong." I looked down at my gloved hands. They were shaking.

"Let's get the hell out of here," said Max, slamming the car door shut. "What the fuck was going on with that guy?" He stared at the man as Jude slowly pulled the car off the forecourt.

"Some messed up rapist – that's what," said Jude, shaking his head. "Any hole will do him – no one's safe around that freak."

Max shuddered. "Are you two okay?" he turned in his seat. "Did he hurt you?"

"No, just shook me up." I forced a smile. If anything like that had happened to me before my night at Cruor Pharma then I would have been mortified, but now, I just felt numb and shaky. I flinched as Raven threw a chocolate bar onto my lap.

"Where did you get...?" I started.

"From the shop," she mumbled. "It's the least that old guy could do for just standing there watching. I'm sure he won't miss a few chocolate bars." She handed two more out to Max and peeled back a wrapper and tucked in.

"Mmmm, this is good," said Jude over a mouthful of chocolate. "I don't know about you lot, but I've got the right munchies."

As if the sight of chocolate suddenly

reminded me that I hadn't eaten since having the stew on Ward 2, my stomach immediately started to rumble. I took a bite and sat quietly.

"I'm not getting out of this car now, until we reach the Bishop's," mumbled Raven. "You can't even go out in broad daylight without some perv trying to rape you in a freaking shop. He was evil – vile."

For once no one argued with Raven. That uneasy feeling was snaking its way up through my body. The man was more than just a rapist. I knew it, deep down inside. I had just come across one of those demons that Ben had told me about – lone demons that wander around, looking for a better body to dwell in, and just like Ben had said, with VA20 now in me, I would be more attractive to them – I had a body that they could live in forever. But how many of these lone demons were there? How could you tell which person was just human and which was demon? Did you have to wait until they tried to attack you? Did some of these demons come across as being nice – fool you into trusting them - then when you let your guard down – they got you – took you by surprise? I looked out through the back window. The man still hadn't left the petrol station. The road lay empty.

"Let's put some distance between us and

that molesting piece of shit," said Jude, pressing down on the accelerator and switching the radio on. He fiddled with the dial until he got a signal – *Changing* by Sigma was playing.

I watched as the petrol station disappeared from view. I wanted to get to the Bishop's house as soon as possible. I needed a break. A break from all those who wanted to dwell inside of me – only there would I truly be able to rest without fear of losing myself. But what would happen when we moved on? How was I ever going to be able to trust anyone ever again? I couldn't. Not if I wanted to stay alive – stay as me.

"Turn the sound up," I said, resting my head against the window. I shut my eyes. The sound of the music filled the car – made my worries sink to the bottom of my brain - drowning out my thoughts.

CHAPTER FOURTEEN

We arrived at Squire Village. It was midday and the journey had taken longer than we had first thought. It had been difficult to find, tucked away down a narrow lane, hidden from the main road. We had spent nearly an hour driving back and forth. The rain hadn't helped. It fell in heavy sheets, blinding our way. The window wipers worked frantically to clear the downpour and the heaters rumbled full blast against the condensation. The narrow lane led down onto an uneven track, just wide enough for a car to pass. It was lined on both sides with thick overgrown brambles. I opened the window a little and peered out. The rain splashed my face and made me shiver. There was no one about, but then who could blame them in this weather? It was like one of those old villages that time had forgotten. Through the sheets of rain I could just make out some buildings set back off the track. Small country cottages lit up with a warm orange glow that settled my nerves – made this run-down village seem not so bad. We passed by the tiny village post office-shop. A light was on so I guessed it was open for business.

"This place is dead," sighed Jude. "I was hoping that it might have had a pub or somewhere you could get a drink. Looks like I'll be making do with ice-lollies and fizzy pop from the post office."

"We're not here to find a pub," I said. "You're meant to be looking for Dusk Fall Retreat."

"I can't see a freaking thing through this rain," moaned Jude, following the track round to the right. The car lurched over the lumps and down into muddy potholes.

"It can't be too hard to find," said Max, opening his window and looking out. "Just look for the church. The Bishop's house should be right next to it or even connected to it."

"There, what's that?" Raven suddenly said, leaning forward in her seat. There's something poking out from the top of those trees."

I leant over her shoulder and peered out through the open window. A church tower could be seen behind the waving treetops and driving rain.

"Keep following this track, "I said. "It should take us right past the church."

We drove by a small cluster of stone cottages and then to our right, an entrance to St. George's appeared underneath a group of swaying Ash trees. A battered wooden sign wobbled from the force of the rain. The dirty-white lettering read *St. George's Church* and underneath it in smaller writing was *Dusk Fall Retreat.*

I felt a huge sense of relief. We had made it to the Bishop's. Max would hopefully find out more about his brother and then, maybe, we might find out more about these demons.

"Pull over there by that red phone box," I said. "We need to work out what we're going to say before knocking on his door."

"We just tell him the truth," said Max. "If my brother and the other volunteers made it to the Bishop's, then he's not gonna be too shocked by what we tell him – especially if Robert is still here."

"What if your brother never made it here?" said Jude, turning the engine off. "Then what? I think he's gonna be pretty shocked to hear our story. Aren't these religious fanatics reluctant to believe in such things? I mean, isn't he just gonna think we're telling him a load of shit?"

"Is that what *you* still think?" I asked Jude. "You've been very reluctant to even admit that there's more to this than just bent doctors and police. When I told you about what Doctor Fletcher had said to me, you didn't want to know, you just brushed the whole demon stuff away like it was a fairy story."

Jude let out a huge sigh, his fingers tapped quietly on the steering wheel. "I'll be honest with you all – I've never believed in all this paranormal crap but... I have to admit that there's been some unexplainable stuff going on and yeah... I don't have an answer for it. But what I'm trying to say is, that if *I've* found it hard to believe and I've been there with you all, I've seen what you've seen – then I think the Bishop is gonna find it *even harder*."

"I believe," mumbled Raven, over the sound of the rain drumming on the top of the car. "I've always believed. I've been seeing dead people for as long as I can remember. They do exist and so does the devil. Demons are his workers – his hands. They go around causing death – taking people's bodies – tempting them to commit sin – to harm others. They even infest objects."

"And you know all this because...?" Jude sat and glared at Raven, waiting for her response. "Well...? Are you some kind of *demon hunter*?"

"I come from a travelling family," scowled Raven. "My mum is a fortune teller. She reads the tarot cards. She speaks to the dead. I've spent my whole life traveling around the country from fair to fair. Sat inside my mum's tent and listened to her contact the dead. I've seen them and I've heard them – I've grown up with them."

"How did you end up in Cruor Pharma then?" I asked, not because I didn't believe her but because volunteering for a drug trial was a million miles away from fortune telling and tarot cards.

"Yeah – let's face it – you were hardly a willing volunteer," said Jude, his blue eyes narrowed as he stared at Raven. "The doctors had to hold you down before they stuck you with a needle."

"*I got scared*," hissed Raven. "I could sense that there was something bad about that ward – *something evil*."

"So what made you volunteer in the first place?" I asked again. "As shallow as it sounds, I only did it for the money – not because I wanted to help save humanity against disease and death. What did you do it for?"

"My mum was running out of money. Tarot reading at the fairs had dried up. She saw the advert in the local paper for the volunteers needed and said I had to do it." Raven looked away. "I didn't want to, but she said if I didn't, then she wouldn't take me with her when the fair next moved on, which would leave me homeless."

I was about to say to Raven that if one of my parents had asked me to do such a thing, I would have told them no but then I thought about my dad and how I would go and buy him whisky, even though I knew it would kill him one day. I guess that wasn't too dissimilar to Raven doing what her mum asked her to do.

"What sad sap would do that for their mum?" Jude screwed his nose up.

"I was pissed with my mum so I decided to go through with it and keep the money for myself. I wasn't planning on handing the money over to her, not after she threatened to leave me behind. I was gonna use the cash to rent somewhere and then I wouldn't need my mum for anything, ever again," huffed Raven.

"I guess she didn't bother to give you a reading with the old cards before you left for Cruor Pharma?" said Jude.

"What do you mean?" Raven frowned, spinning around to face Jude.

"Well, she couldn't have done — could she?" smiled Jude. "Otherwise, she would have been able to read in those cards that Cruor Pharma was full of demons and you would be injected with something *very unworldly*. No parent would knowingly send their child into something like that."

"She did give me a reading actually," snapped Raven. "She told me I would be rewarded with something better than any money could buy. The cards said I ..."

"Oh give it up, will you," huffed Jude. "If there's any truth in tarot cards then your mum would have seen what was going to happen to you... what was..." He stopped mid-sentence. "Hang on, maybe she really did see what was gonna happen... maybe she didn't give a shit?" Jude folded his arms, a look of satisfaction spread over his face.

"Jude – you're out of order," said Max, glaring at him. "There's no need to be cruel."

"Well – what do you expect? Tarot cards, for fuck's sake – how the hell can you find out what's going to happen to you by looking at a bunch of cards with finger paintings on them – I just think it's a load of crap," said Jude.

"Whether the cards work or not – I don't care," I said. "I'm going on what I've seen – what's happened to me and what I've been told. There is truth in the paranormal – for that I'm sure. I wouldn't have believed it myself if I hadn't have seen it." Turning to Max, I added, "If the Bishop hasn't seen your brother, he still should have received the letter that Father William stated in his journal he was going to send. He must know something about what's been going on at Cruor

Pharma. He must at least be wondering what happened to Father William."

"I think we should just go and knock on his door instead of just sitting here arguing about tarot cards," sighed Max. "I'm desperate to hear news about my brother."

"Okay, but let's not bombard the guy with too much, too soon," I said. "Let's just take it slow with him – see what his reaction is to what we tell him." I opened the door and got out.

The rain had eased off now, just a fine misty spray. The air smelt of farmyards and damp soil and the only sound was a distant cockerel calling out. I suddenly felt nervous. What if the Bishop wouldn't help us? What would we do? It was too far to travel in one day to Derbyshire where Doctor Langstone worked. We would need somewhere to sleep overnight. I looked at Max. His green eyes keen. He needed to find out about Robert, but what if the news was bad? It would be terrible for him. We would all feel it. Deep down, I believed that all four of us were banking on good news. Good news meant hope for us all – bad news could mean the end of us, and no one wanted to face that.

CHAPTER FIFTEEN

We followed the gravel driveway which twisted beneath the tall Ash trees. It split off into two directions – one leading to the church – the other to Dusk Fall Retreat. The church was hidden from view by the swaying branches, the leaves falling in whispery flutters.

"Wow, look at this place," hushed Max, his eyes wide at the sight of the building which nestled beside two large oak trees and some overgrown rose bushes. "It's huge."

"And old," mumbled Raven. "I hate old houses."

"This place must date back to the 16th century, I reckon," said Jude, staring up at the plum coloured brickwork and its four large chimney stacks.

"It's very domineering." I shuddered, knowing that the last old building I had been in had been full of monsters and everything you could imagine from nightmares.

"Come on, let's knock on the door," said Max. "We can't stand out here all day." He took the lead and stepped up onto the stone steps. A large wooden door with a heavy iron knocker towered over us.

"Ready?" asked Max, his hand hesitated over the knocker. He looked around at us nervously. Strands of his hair fluttered across his face and his lips twisted up into a half-smile. Or was it more a look of hope?

"Do it." I nodded, chewing on my bottom lip. We had made it this far and there was no point whatsoever in turning back.

Raven shoved herself up behind me, like she was using me as some kind of a shield. She crouched down so she was just peering over my shoulder. Her long black hair flapped across my face.

Bang… bang… bang. The iron knocker thudded hard against the door. A gust of wind sent the fallen leaves scattering over the driveway. I looked over my shoulder. That feeling of being watched sent shivers up my spine. *"Please open the door – please hurry up,"* I whispered under my breath.

Bang… bang… Max tried the door again. He was about to knock a third time, when the sound of bolts being pulled open could be heard from the other side of the door. He stepped back, his eyes wide. I looked at Jude. He stood quite casually, like he didn't give a shit about what or who was behind the door. The wind ruffled up his black hair and he calmly smoothed it down, then ran his hands down the front of his blue shirt like he was trying to iron out the creases. His eyes fell upon me and he winked – not his usual flirty wink but more of a reassuring wink – like I had no need to worry, *I'll look after you* kind of wink.

I looked back at the door as it slowly opened. It creaked and groaned like it hadn't been used for years. A pale face appeared from behind it.

"Can I help you?" A woman in her mid-fifties with ash-blonde hair stood in the doorway. She wore an apron over a patterned dress and a pair of glasses hung from a cord around her neck. Was this the Bishop's wife? Did they have wives? I wasn't sure.

"Hi," smiled Max, showing a set of white teeth. "We were wondering if we could speak with the Bishop." He shoved his hands into his pockets.

"I'm afraid he only sees people if they have made an appointment," said the lady, about to shut the door.

"Please... wait," said Max. "It's very urgent that we speak with him... we've come a long way and we need his help."

"I'm very sorry, but... he's not here." The

lady forced a smile and looked back over her shoulder into the house. "If you call the bishop and make an appointment over the phone then I'm sure he'll be able to see you sometime next week."

"Next week?!" I piped in. "We can't wait until next week – we need to see him *now*."

"Please," said Max. "I need to ask him about my brother, Robert. Do you know if Robert came here?"

"The bishop's work is his private affairs, I am only his housekeeper," said the lady.

"Do you remember seeing this man?" asked Max, pulling out Robert's passport and opening it up on the photo. "Did he come here?"

The lady almost seemed to flinch, a flash of recognition lit up her eyes. "No... no... never seen him before," she said. "It seems that you've had a wasted journey. Maybe your brother went to another church?"

"No, he was told to come here," said Max.

"By whom?" she asked, her eyes wandered over to Jude and Raven like she was checking us out.

"Father William," I answered, stepping forward.

Her mouth dropped open and she looked back again over her shoulder into the hall. "The bishop is very busy and so am I," she said. "I suggest you try another church or go back and speak with Father William." She pushed the door shut.

"Father William is dead!" I shouted through the door, I waited for her response – nothing – the door remained closed. "Now what?"

"Let's go back to the car," said Jude. "We'll talk about it there."

I looked at Max. He stood at the top of the steps – lost. His usual happy green eyes now sad and full of disappointment.

"Come on, Max," I whispered, taking his hand. "We'll find a way to see the bishop, even if it means breaking into his house."

CHAPTER SIXTEEN

We sat in the car - Hannah's hamper perched on my lap. It had stopped raining now, and the sun's rays twinkled through the Ash trees.

"What did she pack?" asked Jude, rubbing his hands together. "I'm starving."

"Chicken vol au vents and potato salad," I answered, staring at the food. I placed the pot of potato salad onto the top of the hamper so everyone could reach it.

"What the hell are chicken vol au vents?" mumbled Raven, turning her nose up at them.

"Does it matter?" I raised my voice. "Its food, isn't it? Be grateful you've got this."

Raven shut up as soon as she saw the look on my face and took a bite of the vol au vent. "It's okay... I guess."

"Right, what are we going to do next?" I said, taking a bite of the vol au vent. "You know... I can't eat this. Hannah made it and I just can't face it." I opened the window and threw the vol au vent out. My hunger had suddenly disappeared. It didn't feel right to be sitting here eating food that Hannah had made just before her death.

Max, who was just about to take a bite,

changed his mind after seeing the look on my face and placed the vol au vent back down. "You're right, I can't eat it either."

"Can't let it go to waste," said Jude, grabbing a handful of Hannah's food. "I'll eat it." He forked in several large mouthfuls of potato salad, completely oblivious to my feelings.

Trying to ignore his tactless behaviour, I said, "That housekeeper recognised your brother's photo, I'm sure of that. You could see it in her eyes. She's hiding something."

"Yeah, she's got some little secret alright, we'll have to knock again and refuse to leave," said Jude, popping in a whole vol au vent into his mouth. "She'll have to let us in."

"What if she calls the police?" said Max. "We don't want Inspector Cropper turning up here."

"It's a risk we'll have to take," said Jude. "I don't think she will. I don't think her or the bishop want the police sniffing round. My guess is that they know what's been going on at Cruor Pharma but they've kept quiet about it – probably scared that the same shit that happened to the other volunteers would happen to them if they went public." Jude took the flask of tea and poured himself a cup. "I bet Doctor Middleton isn't even aware that the bishop knows what he's been up to. Let's face it – if he did, then the housekeeper and the bishop wouldn't even be alive. The cleaners would have disposed of them by now – just like Nurse Jones's son was dealt with. They cover their tracks. It seems that Cruor Pharma keeps everyone on a tight leash – and we know why."

I thought back to when Max and I had been trying to walk out through the main gate to escape the hospital. The workers in front of me had been talking about the murder of Fred Butler when a maintenance guy had told them to stop talking about it. *"What goes on in here stays in here."* I could clearly hear his voice like I was back there, attempting to get past the security guards at the gate.

"Those workers have been led to believe that it was us who killed Fred, Nurse Jones, and the other volunteers. Even they don't realise what's really going on," I said. "It's like a secret within a secret. The workers keep quiet about the drug trials – thinking that they've just gone wrong – want to keep their jobs, so they never discuss Cruor Pharma to the outside world. And then you've got the doctors who are keeping secret what's really happening and what they truly are."

"I bet there have been some workers

who've let things slip and have disappeared off the face of the earth," said Max. "Can Cruor Pharma really keep everyone quiet?"

"Well they've done a good enough job of it so far," hissed Raven. "Two sets of drug trials have resulted in two groups of volunteers escaping – we're one group, and your brother is a part of the other one. I don't remember hearing anything about your brother's escape on the news – do you?"

Max shook his head. "But how do they get away with it? I mean, all those volunteers who have died must have had family – their parents must have wondered what happened to their sons and daughters. I don't get it? So many missing people – yet not one mention on the news or in the papers."

"Well I'm not missed," I said. "Both my parents are dead. The only one who knew about me going into Cruor Pharma was Hannah." I looked out the window as the mention of her name brought unwanted images of her death.

The car fell silent.

"I don't mean to sound heartless or tactless, Kassidy," began Max. "But Hannah's no longer a problem to Middleton. She can't come looking for you or go to the press when there's no sign of you

– she's dead – she's dealt with – no one is ever gonna ask where's Kassidy gone."

"Well what about you?" Is there anyone missing you?" I asked. "And you, Jude."

"My parents died in a car crash. Robert is the only family I have now," said Max. "But he's been missing for three months now, so he's not gonna be missing me and going to the police. So I guess Middleton doesn't need to worry about anyone asking questions about my disappearance."

I looked at Jude. "Do you have parents?"

"Somewhere," he shrugged. "I left home ages ago. My mum's dead and my dad couldn't be bothered with me – too busy with his work to spare me even a glance in the morning when I left for college. Work-work-work was all he was ever interested in. I was just an interruption to his life – a hindrance to his ever-important work. So I left and he never came looking for me."

"Well your mum is gonna wonder where you've gone," I said, staring at Raven. "When you don't go back to her today, she's gonna start asking questions."

"Is she?" said Jude. "Sounds to me like mummy knew what she was doing. I guess she saw Raven's future and pushed her in the right direction – that is if we are to believe in the power

152

of the tarot cards."

"You're just saying that because your own dad couldn't stand the sight of *you*," spat Raven. "You can't bear the thought of someone else having parents who love them."

"So mummy is gonna go to the police about her missing daughter, or is it just that she wants the money that you were meant to get from the drug trial? Maybe that's the only thing she's gonna miss," said Jude, glaring at Raven, his top lip curled up in a grimace.

"Enough!" I shouted. "This isn't some fucking competition about who has the most loving parents. Can't you see that there's a bit of a pattern here? I think Middleton only picks volunteers who have no family – you know, loners, young people whose parents are dead or have drifted apart from each other. I think Doctor Middleton knew all this information about our family backgrounds. He must have checked us all out – been watching us – hand-picking the people who answered that advert in the local paper – the ones who had no one to love them, the people who would be least missed."

I shuddered at the thought. I didn't like the idea that I had been snooped on, and not just by any old person but by some evil, twisted demon.

Middleton must have known who my dad was. Known that he was one of his workforce at some point and even that didn't stop him from picking me – there was obviously no honour amongst Cruor Pharma and its workers – but then did that really surprise me? He had already ordered the murder of Nurse Jones's son and she had worked quite closely with Middleton. He didn't give a shit about his workforce. That was plainly obvious.

"If you're right about this," said Jude, "then how come they picked Max's brother? They would have seen that Robert had a younger brother living with him – they wouldn't have risked it, surely?"

"I wasn't living with Robert at the time he volunteered," said Max. "I was living with my girlfriend."

"But they must have done a check on Robert's family background," said Jude, taking a slurp of his tea. "They would have seen that he had a brother – a brother who would start asking questions."

"Which you did," I said, looking at Max. "You went straight to Holly Tree police station."

"I'm surprised Inspector Cropper didn't deal with you there and then," said Jude.

"I think if I had been persistent then I probably wouldn't be here now," said Max, watching Jude work his way through the food like a Hoover sucking up every last crumb.

"That still doesn't explain how Robert got picked when he had a younger brother though," I said. "Knowing how tight Cruor Pharma are on keeping their secrets – somehow you seem to have slipped through their net."

Max sat with a frown over his face, then, as if suddenly coming up with the winning lottery ticket, his eyes widened and lit up. Pulling out Robert's passport he waved it in the air. "If they did look into mine and Robert's family history, I guess they wouldn't have made a connection between us. Robert doesn't share the same surname as me. I'm a *Landy* and he's an *O'Brien*. It's a long story – but my dad had an affair years ago. Robert never took the name Landy – he kept his mother's maiden name, even though he lost contact with her – his way of hanging onto the only thing he had left of her, I guess."

"Well that probably explains it then," I said. "And reinforces my theory on young people getting picked who appear to have no family or family that have nothing to do with their children."

"Maybe, I'm too tired to even think about it," said Max, yawning, "My brain feels fried. I was kind of hoping that we'd be inside the bishop's house by now – finding out where Robert is and getting some sleep without fear that the cleaners would turn up."

I looked at the clock on the dashboard. We had been sat in the car for nearly an hour watching Jude devour the food like a tornado. Maybe it was time to head back up that gravel driveway and approach the housekeeper again. After all, time was short and the mention of the cleaners had my heart racing again.

CHAPTER SEVENTEEN

We stood outside the front door to the bishop's house. The wind had picked up, howling through the trees, and the branches looked like a hundred arms performing the Mexican wave.

As Max was about to knock, the net curtain at the large bay window twitched and the housekeeper's face appeared. She mouthed through the window for us to go away.

"No!" I shouted through the window. "We need to see the bishop and we're not leaving until we speak with him."

The housekeeper looked behind her as if making sure she was alone and then opened the window. "I've already told you, the bishop is busy. Please – you should leave," she whispered, almost begged.

"I'm not going until I find out whether my brother came here and where he went after," said Max.

"The bishop isn't…" she started then got cut short by a loud male voice coming from behind her.

"Who are you talking to, Mrs. Gables?"

She turned away from the window and disappeared from view behind the net curtain.

"That must be the bishop," mumbled Raven, peering out from under her black hair. "I don't like the sound of his voice."

"I don't think Mrs. Gables likes the sound of his voice either," said Jude. "She looked pretty shaken when she heard him."

"What should we do?" I said, gripping the strap of Father Williams's satchel as a gust of wind blew it from off my shoulder.

As if in answer to my question, the large wooden door slowly creaked open and Mrs. Gables appeared in her patterned dress and apron. She looked nervous – eyes flitted over each of us – her bottom lip trembled and she stood to the side and said, "Come in. The bishop will see you."

"Thanks," said Max, stepping past the housekeeper.

I followed the others through the front door and found myself standing in a huge hallway with a grand oak staircase. The room felt cold with its large stone slabs covering the floor. They looked worn in places like it had had countless feet pass over it through the many years this house had stood. A collection of old tapestries hung from the walls and a fire roared in a hearth with some kind of brass bucket containing a large pile of coal next to it.

"Follow me," said Mrs. Gables, locking the front door and heading across the hall.

She led us through a small hallway and stopped outside a door. Knocking gently, she turned and said, "Go in, the bishop is waiting for you." She turned away and headed back down the hallway, nervously peering over her shoulder at us before disappearing from view.

Her strange behaviour left me feeling anxious, like the bishop was someone to fear. But he was a man of god, and after spending a night at Cruor Pharma with men filled with nothing but evil, I told myself that nothing or no one could be worse than them.

"Enter," the bishop's voice sounded from behind the door.

We looked at each other – unsure as to whether this was the right thing to do or maybe I wasn't the only one feeling anxious after Mrs. Gable's timid behaviour?

"You go first," whispered Jude, pushing Raven forward.

"No way," hissed Raven, stepping to the side and repositioning herself at the back. "He sounds angry."

"I'll go." Max and I spoke at the same time, our hands both reached out for the door handle.

He looked at me with a smile.

"Ladies first then." He stepped away from the door and straightened up his jacket.

Taking a deep breath, I turned the handle and pushed open the door. The bishop sat behind a worn wooden desk. His long white beard looked like a mass of cottonweed with eyebrows to match. He wore a pale blue shirt which, was undone at the neck, and a thick Aran cardigan.

"Please, take a seat," he said, looking at each of us in turn. "Mrs. Gables informs me that you needed to speak with me on a matter of urgency."

"Yes we do," I said, sitting down. The room was cold and I shuddered. There was no fireplace in here and no central heating.

"Well, how can I help you?" asked the bishop, leaning forward and placing his hands on the desk. "What brings four young people to my house? It's not often I get visitors here. The village is pretty remote and it's usually just the local members of my church who visit me."

"I'm looking for my brother, Robert O'Brien," said Max, who had taken the seat next to me. "We think he came here for help."

"And what makes you believe such a thing?" said the bishop, straightening up in his chair. "Why would your brother come here?"

"Because Father William told him to come here," I said, opening up the satchel and pulling out Father Williams's journal. "It says so in here."

The bishop held out his hand and took the journal from me. Flicking through the pages, he said, "Where did you find this?"

"In the chapel at Cruor Pharma," I answered, "I found it beside..."

The bishop suddenly stood up and walked over to the window. He stood with his back to us. I looked over at Jude and Raven who had each taken the sofa by the door. Raven sat hunched forward, her hair draped over her face.

"Continue," the bishop said, still staring out the window, his hands laced behind his back.

"I found it beside Father Williams's body," I said, feeling uncomfortable about giving him such news. I waited for his response – half expecting him to swing around – shocked – upset even. But there was no such reaction. It almost seemed like he already knew.

"So... you are all from Cruor Pharma, are you?" he said, slowly turning around to face us. His eyes had narrowed and his cottonweed eyebrows almost seemed to swallow them up. "I would like you to all leave – now."

"What?" said Max. "Why? We came here for your help – for answers. I don't under…"

"I can't give you any help," the bishop cut him off. "I don't help people from Cruor Pharma – I don't want anything to do with its workers, its doctors or anything else for that matter. Go – *now*."

Jude stood up. "Hey, just calm down. You seem to think that we work for Cruor Pharma – well, we don't. We were volunteers for one of Doctor Middleton's so-called drug trials and we escaped. I've driven all the way out here because Max is looking for his brother and we need somewhere to stay – somewhere safe. That's all we ask."

The bishop stood quietly for a moment, like he was working things out in his head – putting together what Jude had just told him. "How do I believe you've not been sent here by Doctor Middleton? That this isn't some kind of attempt to get at me? To find out what I really know about Cruor Pharma and its doctors?"

"Because of this," hissed Raven, standing up and pulling the sleeve of Hannah's leather jacket up. "People who work for Cruor Pharma don't have black veins filled with *devil's liquid* or whatever it's called – no, they leave that for all the poor, unsuspecting volunteers to be injected with."

The bishop's eyes widened at the sight of Raven's veins but didn't seem overly shocked by it. It seemed to me that he had seen it all before, which meant that Robert had probably come here.

"You've seen others like this, haven't you?" I said, standing up. "We're not the first to come here with veins filled with VA20."

"Is that what it's called now?" said the bishop, taking his seat again, "The last group of people who turned up here called it VA10. This must be some kind of new batch that Middleton and Wright have concocted."

"So you know what's been going on at Cruor Pharma," I said, still standing. "You've seen Max's brother?"

"I have," he answered, getting out of his chair again and walking over to something which looked like a cord hanging down from the ceiling. He pulled on it. A distant chime rang out and moments later, Mrs. Gables entered the room.

"Have the dining table set for five tonight please, Mrs. Gables, and make up some beds for our guests. They will be staying for a while." The bishop turned to face us. "We have plenty to talk about, but let's save it for over dinner."

CHAPTER EIGHTEEN

The lounge which led off from the main hallway was cold, just like the bishop's study. Its large bay window looked out onto the gravel driveway, and as I peered out I could see that it was beginning to get dark. Large rain clouds were gathering, rolling across the sky, pushed on by the wind. I sat down on the window seat and waited for Jude to appear. He had gone back to his car with the intention of bringing it up to the house. Leaving it on the roadside was not a good idea. If one of the villagers reported the car being left there then it might alert Inspector Cropper to where we were.

"Do you think we're safe here?" asked Max, sitting on a leather armchair that looked like it had a set of wings on the back.

"I hope so," I said, wrapping my arms about me. "If we're not safe here, then I guess we're not safe anywhere."

"Do you think we'd be better off sleeping in the church?" said Max. "I mean, it's probably holier than in the bishop's house – we might be more protected there."

"I'm not sleeping in the church," mumbled

Raven pulling over a heavy-looking armchair covered in red silk. "The dead are always hanging around churches. We've got enough dead things following us, we don't need a *freaking party* of them."

"I think we'll be all right here," I said, looking around at the antique furniture which dressed the room. The house smelt like an old stately home – one you might visit on a day trip. "I just wish it was warmer in here – or Mrs. Gables would come in and light the fire." I walked over to the open fireplace. It was filled with a stack of dusty coals, and I wondered how long ago they had been placed in there. Judging by the amount of dust over them, it was obvious that this room wasn't used often. I crouched down and looked up the chimney. It had been boarded over. Maybe they had no need for it as it appeared that the room wasn't much lived in. I sat back on the window seat and rubbed my arms for warmth.

"I wonder what the bishop will tell us?" sighed Max. "I hope it's good news about my brother. This is the closest I've got to finding out what's happened to him and where he is."

"Why did Robert volunteer himself for a drug trial?" I asked. "Did he do it for the money?"

"He wanted the money to set up a business.

We were gonna run it together – painting and decorating," said Max. "He knew how difficult it was to find work in Holly Tree and thought that the only way of earning money was to start up our own business." Max stared up at the ceiling and sighed. "I wish I'd stopped him. When he told me about volunteering up at Cruor Pharma, I should have told him not to do it – but I didn't."

"You weren't to know, Max," I said. "None of us knew what we were getting into."

"If only we could turn back the clock, eh?" Max said. "Wipe away our mistakes, regrets."

"Fuck-ups," Raven piped in. "If I could turn back the clock, I'd stop it where you lot stood and watched those monsters inject me on Ward 2." Raven shifted in her seat, arms crossed tightly over her chest and her dark eyes glaring from me to Max.

I looked back out through the window. I didn't want to get into another row with Raven. Too much had happened. I felt like a machine that had been given too much information and was on the brink of shutting down – folding. I needed to turn off – cool down – unplug myself. Rest for a while in standby mode until all the backlogged information had processed and only then would I be able to run at full speed. It was no use me sitting here, thinking about Doctor Middleton, the cleaners, Hannah, the police, and that freak at the petrol station. My head was full to bursting and getting into another row with Raven might just push me into meltdown.

"Jude's back," said Max. He had stood up and was now standing next to me, watching Jude park the car underneath the swaying branches of the Ash trees. He placed his hand on my shoulder and squeezed it gently. He bent over me and whispered into my ear, "Don't let her get to you. Raven's just messed up – like the rest of us."

I placed my hand over Max's and squeezed back. Looking up into his face like it was the first time I had seen him, I realised how handsome he was. I hadn't noticed it before, but then we had all been on the run – escape the only thing going through our heads. Now I could see him – the chase had slowed a little – time allowing me to take in more of my surroundings – more of the people I was with. His kind green eyes stared down at me and his lips turned up a little as a warm smile appeared. I suddenly wanted to pull him down – my hands holding his face - my lips pressed against his. The feel of his blonde hair brushing against my skin – his strong hands holding me tight. I broke my gaze and stared back out of the window. Did I really feel like this for Max? Or was I just in need of some love – some company – security? Someone to take me away from all this horror and give me that human touch that I suddenly craved? My thoughts turned to Ben. I could still feel his hands on me – smell him – see the stubble shading the lower half of his face. Those blue-crystal eyes eating me up as his fingers slipped under the hospital gown I had worn, making my skin melt with his smouldering touch. I closed my eyes as I remembered the soft brush of his lips over mine. But was that Ben? Hadn't it been his demon who had held me in a trance-like state? Hadn't it been the demon who had touched me and made me want him? I didn't really know what to think anymore, so I stood up and tried to push away all those sudden desires that were filling me up. Now really wasn't the time to start jumping into bed with the nearest guy. I had way too many problems going on and I didn't need a moment of recklessness to add to them.

CHAPTER NINETEEN

The savoury aroma of dinner seeped into the lounge overshadowing the old stately house smell that seemed to linger like time had stood still. I felt my stomach rumble and my mouth watered at the heavenly scent that filled the air.

Mrs. Gables appeared at the door, an unsure look over her face as she looked at us. "Dinner is ready. If you follow me, I'll show you to your seats."

She led us across the large hall. It seemed that every couple of seconds she would glance over her shoulder nervously at us and speed up if we got too close.

Stepping to the side of a wooden door, she said, "The bishop will be with you soon. Go in and sit down." She backed away from us and disappeared through another doorway.

A mahogany dining table big enough to seat six, was covered with several china serving bowls and five placemats. We each took a seat and left the head of the table free for the bishop. The dining table was positioned by a set of French doors leading out into the garden. The room had been lit with some candles and a small fire crackled in the hearth, making the room warm and cosy. Every couple of minutes the sound of rain hitting the French doors would fill the room with a clatter, like gravel being thrown at glass. I looked across the table at Jude and Raven. A decanter of wine seemed to have caught Jude's attention as he ran his fingers over a wine glass that was placed beside his dinner plate. Max sat next to me. He had taken the seat beside where the bishop would sit.

"Don't you think you should take your jackets off?" said Jude, looking at Max and then Raven. "We are having dinner with a bishop after all."

"I can hardly eat dinner with a bishop with no shirt on, Jude," said Max. "I think that would look worse, don't you?"

Jude nodded his head as if in agreement with Max and then turned to Raven. "What about you? You're wearing that pretty flowered blouse – you've got no excuse."

"I'm not taking the jacket off," huffed Raven. "I don't like the blouse and you know it – so quit trying to wind me up." She zipped the jacket up tight to her neck as if in defiance and stared blankly up at the ceiling.

"Suit yourself," shrugged Jude. "I wonder what Mrs. Gables has cooked us?" He patted his stomach. "I could eat a horse."

"How do we know she hasn't put poison in it?" hissed Raven. "It's *obvious* she doesn't want us here."

"Sshh," said Max. He frowned at Raven. "Keep your voice down. I don't want to get thrown out of here before I've even heard anything about my brother."

"Yeah, try to be pleasant," said Jude. "I know it's hard for you but just try."

The door to the dining room swung open and the bishop walked in and took his seat. Mrs. Gables followed behind him.

"Is there anything else you need?" she asked, looking at the bishop, her hands clasped tightly in front of her.

"That will be all, Mrs. Gables," smiled the bishop. "When dinner is over you can retire for the night."

Mrs. Gables left the room, closing the door behind her. We looked at the bishop. An uncomfortable silence hung in the air. It felt strange to be sitting down for dinner with a complete stranger. Holy man or not, I wondered why Mrs. Gables seemed so on edge around him. Why had she tried to hide our appearance from him when we had first turned up at his home?

"Please, help yourself," said the bishop, standing up and passing one of the serving bowls to Max. "Mrs. Gables is a very fine cook and I'm sure you must all be very hungry."

Max took the lid off of the bowl and a flurry of steam wafted up. He took a large spoonful of peas and carrots and passed the bowl across to Jude.

After filling our plates with Shepherd's Pie and vegetables topped off with some gravy, the bishop cleared his throat and said, "You wanted to know about your brother, Robert?"

"Yes," answered Max, his mouth full of food.

"Your brother did come here." The bishop put his knife and fork down and poured himself a glass of red wine from the decanter. "He was in a terrible state, as were the other two who were with him. At first I thought that they were drunk or on some kind of hallucination drug. But when I let them into my home in the light from the lamps, I saw their veins. When your brother started talking about Father William and Cruor Pharma, I knew they were telling me the truth. Just one mention of Cruor Pharma was enough to open my eyes and ears."

"How come?" I asked. "Had you heard

things before about Cruor Pharma?"

The bishop took a large gulp of wine and then wiped his lips with a napkin. "Father William wasn't the first priest that I sent to Cruor Pharma. Before him I had sent Father Benet and after him, Father Peter. They both left their posts earlier than planned. Neither of them liked serving the chapel at Cruor Pharma, and when I questioned them about it, they were very reluctant to tell me of their concerns. I didn't understand what the problem could be. After all, I knew that Father William had served the chapel many years before them and he'd never had one complaint against Cruor Pharma. After some persuading, Father Benet told me that he didn't like the feel of the place. He said it was like something hung over Cruor Pharma, like a blanket of despair, and that the staff had become very vacant. When Doctor Middleton closed the old part of the hospital, Father Benet asked to be moved to another parish. He felt that there was little need for him now that there would be no patients and the hospital had moved more into research. He seemed very unhappy, so I agreed to move him."

"Is that why you sent Father Peter – to fill the vacancy?" I asked.

"Yes. Just because there were no more

patients to visit, didn't mean I could turn my back on Cruor Pharma. After all, there was still the chapel and I think, back then, I believed that maybe Father Benet just hadn't been right for that posting." The bishop stood up and poured himself another glass of wine. "How rude of me, I haven't offered you all a glass, would you like some?"

"Yes please." Jude smiled and held up his glass. His eyes lit up as the red liquid poured in. "Thanks." He took several large gulps and then wiped his mouth with the back of his hand. "That's good."

"Italian, I think," smiled the bishop, offering the wine to Raven.

She screwed her nose up and shook her head, "No, I don't like red wine, it looks like blood."

The bishop moved round to me and Max, and without asking us he filled our glasses. "Now, where was I? Ah yes, Father Peter."

"Why did Father Peter not like it there?" asked Max, taking a sip of the wine.

"He had only been at Cruor Pharma for two weeks when he came to visit me here at Dusk Fall Retreat. He was very pale and... how should I put it? On edge," said the bishop, nodding to himself. "He asked if he could be placed elsewhere. I asked him why, and he said that he felt very unwelcome at Cruor Pharma. I remember my response to him was the Lord's work is difficult at times and not everyone is ready to receive Him. I told Father Peter that he must be patient – not everyone goes to church and those who don't may still believe but they worship our Lord in different ways."

"And what did he say to that?" I asked, placing my knife and fork down on my plate.

"He took no comfort in my words and fell to his knees – pleading that I move him," said the bishop, his wiry eyebrows raised. "When I pushed him further to explain his outburst, he simply said that there were terrible things going on at Cruor Pharma. Rumours amongst the staff regarding six coffins and a drug that turned normal healthy people into monsters."

"Did you believe him?" I asked, watching the bishop wipe his mouth, flecks of his dinner caught up in his beard.

The bishop shook his head and paused for a moment before answering me. "I had never been witness to anything otherworldly at that time and I never wanted to even contemplate that such evil could really exist. So instead of facing it, I did the easiest thing and that was to agree to move Father Peter and try to brush off the disturbing things he had told me." The bishop finished the last of his wine and poured himself another glass. "It's one of my biggest regrets that I didn't do more. When Father Peter left Dusk Fall Retreat that afternoon, he threw himself in front of a train."

"He was really messed up," said Jude. "Poor guy."

"Witnesses say they saw Father Peter struggling with himself – almost fighting something along the platform – like he didn't want to throw himself onto the tracks but then he did," said the bishop. "It was reported that Father Peter's last words were something like – *'They've come to kill me – they know I've spoken against them – Trabek has sent his servants.'* I don't know." The bishop shook his head. "I can't quite remember exactly what was said and I'm sure the witnesses were somewhat disturbed, so they could have got it wrong but..."

"Trabek?" said Max. "Who's that?"

"At the time I had no idea," said the bishop, knocking back another gulp of his wine. "But I decided to do a little research on Cruor Pharma and this Trabek."

"What did you find?" Raven suddenly piped in. "Devil worshippers and human sacrifices?"

"Not quite, my dear. I have access to records and archives of my diocese – my parish," said the bishop, standing up and walking over to the French doors. "They contain such things as baptisms, marriages, burials, and deaths, and date back years and years. I found Doctor Middleton's marriage recorded in these archives and the baptism of his son. All seems perfectly normal – you might think, only... his age doesn't add up. The date his son was baptised doesn't add up either."

"How do you mean?" asked Jude, helping himself to another glass of wine.

"Well, Doctor Middleton shouldn't even be alive – the dates put him at being well over a hundred and sixty years old now, and his son would be dead also. So does that mean that we have two people taking on the identity of Middleton and his son, or do we have something very otherworldly going on?"

The wind suddenly picked up throwing the rain against the glass. It howled an eerie wail through the old house making the door to the dining room open. We all jumped. The bishop spun around, a look of concern across his face. When he realised that there was no one at the door, he sat down.

I thought about what he had just told us. It wasn't really anything surprising – just a confirmation about what we had already gathered from Father Williams's journal. I was about to say so when the bishop started talking again.

"His wife's death is recorded also," said the bishop, "she died when the son would have been in his late teens. It states that she was murdered."

"By whom?" I asked, taking a sip of wine.

"The murderer was never found," said the bishop, her body had been hacked to pieces. A very unpleasant affair."

Jude reached across the table and poured the last of the wine into his glass. "What about this Trabek? What did you find out about him or her?"

"Not too much. I have a very old book in my library and the name Trabek is mentioned in it," said the bishop, "under the section about demons."

"We already know that demons are involved in all this," I said, feeling rather frustrated. I had hoped that the bishop might have had something new to tell us.

"Well, alongside this demon named Trabek are five other demons mentioned. It says that a group of servants travel with theses otherworldly creatures and it is believed that whichever demon can find a suitable body for the servants, then those servants will obey that demon and *only* that demon. When this has been successfully achieved, only then can the demon summon other servants who are yet to enter our world," said the bishop, pushing his plate away. "It sounds like something you would watch in a movie, I know, but after everything I have heard and seen, it worries me greatly that these creatures are real and planning on infesting our world and our people."

"Can you remember the names of the five other demons?" I asked, taking a sip of wine.

The bishop sat quietly for a moment, his fingers twiddled through his beard as he tried to remember. "Eras... Trabek... Quint... Doshia..." He shook his head. "I can't remember the other two names off the top of my head, I will have to take another look at the book."

"Doshia," said Max, turning to look at us. "That's what Hannah said."

I leant back in my seat. With each piece of new information, not only did it give me answers but it also gave me new fears. Deep down I was still hoping that this was just one big nightmare and I would wake up. Instead it just reinforced the true horror that I was caught up in and the realisation that although I had escaped Cruor Pharma, there was no escaping the demons. I could run from them – keep moving from place to place - but I couldn't run from myself. I looked down at the black veins on my hands. How could I get away from what was inside me? Wherever I went, the demons in me would come too.

CHAPTER TWENTY

We had left the dining room and were now seated in a room that the bishop called the snug. A large fire burned in the hearth and I sat with my legs curled up on one end of a tatty-looking sofa. The bishop had seated himself in a large armchair by the window, the curtains pulled tight. Max and Raven had taken the other sofa, and Jude sat on the floor, propped up against the sofa where I sat. The walls almost seemed to be moving as the shadows from the fire danced across them.

"So, can you tell me about my brother?" asked Max, looking at the bishop. "How was he? Did he look like us? Black veins and twisted nails?"

"Yes," answered the bishop. "He had thick black veins and seemed to have a fever. But the other two were in a worse state than him."

"In what way?" asked Raven, twisting a strand of her hair around her finger. "Did they try and eat you?"

"No, they appeared traumatized – disturbed," said the bishop. "They were both covered in black veins and their skin had a sickly-grey colour about it. The young lady, Sylvia, was extremely distressed. There was no calming her.

Your brother Robert had to hold her down. He begged me to perform an exorcism but I knew there was little point. They hadn't been possessed – just drugged with something terrible. I remember suggesting that I call for an ambulance but your brother wouldn't hear of it. After he explained that they had come from Cruor Pharma, and that Father Williams had sent them, I understood why they didn't want an ambulance. Memories of what had happened to Father Peter was enough to stop me from contacting anyone. I had become convinced that if you spoke out about Cruor Pharma or the doctors then something bad would happen to you. I am ashamed to say that I wished that your brother and his two companions hadn't come here. I felt they had put me in danger – placed me in a rather difficult situation – one that I didn't want to be associated with."

I slumped back on the sofa. I had hoped that maybe the bishop could perform an exorcism on us – rid us of this dark matter that infested our veins – but that hope had now been crushed.

"Well I guess you must have done a good job in keeping their appearance here pretty quiet," said Max. "After all, you're still here and nothing bad has happened to you."

"Well, I thought I had done a good job in

hiding the fact that they had come here, but here you all are, so... I hadn't contemplated that Father William would write about it in a journal." The bishop forced a smile. "Does anyone else know that you were coming here?"

"Just one," I whispered, thinking of Hannah, "but she's dead, so you don't need to worry about it." I looked up at a painting which hung above the fireplace and wished I could step into it and disappear. It had two old train carriages pulled in at a smoky-looking station. Passengers were waiting on the platform with suitcases ready to embark on a journey. If only I could be one of those people – leave this life behind and start a new one at the end of the train line, wherever that may be. I looked at the bishop. I understood how he felt. He wanted to cover any trace, any association with the victims of Cruor Pharma so nothing would come and get him. He was right to feel this way. Hannah had been dealt with, Father Williams silenced, and the same had happened to Nurse Jones and her son. But if Robert, Sylvia, and Alex had been here and had left and no harm had come to the bishop, then surely we were safe here and so was the bishop.

"So they hadn't turned into crazy zombies then?" asked Raven leaning forward in her seat, "they were like us but a bit more messed up?"

I looked at Raven, surprised by her sudden interest. She hadn't seemed to be concerned in anything, really, other than ghosts and demons. Now she seemed to be engrossed in finding out about Max's brother and the other two volunteers.

"They were in a bad way," answered the bishop, looking at Raven. "But not like zombies."

"Were they sane?" Raven pushed for more details. "You know… did they think straight… did they have full control over themselves?"

"Raven, why are you so interested all of a sudden?" I asked.

"Because if their normal, then we'll stay normal," she said. "And if we find them then we'll be stronger – you know… safety in numbers."

"What happened to them?" asked Jude. "Where did they go?"

"They stayed here for a few days and then they left for Derbyshire – Doctor Langstone's I do believe," said the bishop. "I'm sorry, Max, but I haven't heard from them since."

"So they had the same idea as us," I said, looking at Max. "We know Sylvia never made it to Doctor Langstone's but did your brother and Alex get there?"

"If they did, why hasn't Robert contacted

184

me?" Max slumped back against a cushion. "I feel like I haven't got any further forward in finding Robert. When I get to a place that I know he was at, he's already moved on."

"At least we know that he got out of Cruor Pharma and left here very much alive," I said. "He wasn't caught with Sylvia so there's still hope."

Max nodded his head. "I guess."

"You say you're going to Doctor Langstone's?" asked the bishop, a look of concern over his face. "I don't think that's a very good idea. If you haven't heard from your brother then that could mean that all is not well. If Doctor Langstone had helped Robert and Alex then surely you would have heard from him."

"I agree," said Jude, turning to look up at me. "Doctor Langstone is one of these demons who can't be trusted. I think we should consider our options, don't you?" Jude turned to Max. "We need to find Robert and Alex, but just strolling into Doctor Langstone's place could be the end of us."

"Why don't you stay here?" suggested the bishop. "You are more than welcome. Maybe Robert will come back here when he thinks it's safe?"

"Thanks, but I can't just sit back waiting here in the hope that Robert will turn up," said

Max. "I don't mind staying here for a couple of nights just to rest up a bit but that's it. I've come this far and I'll keep going until I find Robert."

"Besides, we don't know how long we have before the cleaners turn up," I said. "I know we should be safe here but what happens when we leave? What if the cleaners are outside? The moment we step foot out of here – then what? Two nights might be pushing it."

"I don't see the point in staying here at all," grumbled Raven. "We only came here to find Robert and the others. We should leave now and head for Derbyshire before it's too late. I don't want to become a *demon's* puppet."

"We need to sleep, Raven," I said. "We can't keep on going with no rest. Let's stay tonight and then move on tomorrow."

Raven slumped back against the cushion, arms folded tight across her. Her lips turned down into a pout and she glared out at me from under her black hair. I looked at Jude. He had got up and was now peering out through a gap in the curtain. All this talk about the cleaners turning up had probably made him feel on edge, not that he would ever admit it. He turned away from the window. His shiny blue eyes met mine.

"It's not just the cleaners we have to worry

about," he said. "Don't forget the police are after us as well. The cleaners may have trouble getting to us while we're in here but the police won't."

"The police don't know we're here," said Max, leaning forward on the sofa. "I think if they did, then they'd be here by now."

"Maybe, but do we want to take that risk?" said Jude, sitting down on the arm of the sofa beside me. "I really don't know what's the best plan to take."

"I think you all need a good night's sleep," said the bishop, standing up and walking over to another cord that hung from the wall. "Sleep on it and have a serious think about staying here with me and waiting for Robert to come back." He pulled on the cord and a distant bell chimed from somewhere in the house. "Mrs. Gables will show you to your rooms, but please stay away from the third floor. Well, it isn't really a third floor – more of an attic. It's not safe up there. The house is very old, as I'm sure you can tell, and sadly the attic is falling into disrepair. The floorboards up there are rotting away and I wouldn't want any of you falling through them."

The door to the snug opened and Mrs. Gables appeared. She looked nervous again. Her eyes flicked over us and then settled on the bishop.

I couldn't tell if it was us or the bishop she seemed to be scared of. When we had first turned up, I thought it had been the bishop, but now, as she eyed us nervously, it seemed to be our presence that had her looking scared.

"Mrs. Gables, could you show our guests to their rooms please."

"Of course," said Mrs. Gables, nodding her head at the bishop. "Follow me."

We stood up and left the room. Turning around to the bishop who had followed us out, I said, "Thank you for letting us stay."

"I couldn't turn you away," he smiled. "I will help you, like I helped the others. I'll do whatever it takes to keep your being here quiet. After all, it seems that it's not just you and your friends that could get into trouble – now you are all here, then myself and Mrs. Gables could find ourselves suffering the same fate as Father William or Father Peter and I don't want that. I'm just sorry that I can't do more."

As I went to walk away, the bishop spoke again. "Make sure you keep the fire burning in your rooms. The house gets very cold and I like to keep a nice roaring fire burning all the time." He grabbed hold of my arm and peered down at me. His eyebrows lowered so I could barely see his pupils.

"Make sure you tell your friends. *Tell them. Don't let the fires go out.*"

CHAPTER TWENTY ONE

I headed across the large hall to where the others waited for me at the bottom of the oak staircase. That uneasy feeling had started to ebb its way back into my stomach and up my throat. The bishop's request to keep the fires burning was reasonable enough but it had been the way he had grabbed my arm and the persistence in his voice that had disturbed me. I could understand an old man wanting to keep his house warm but he had spoken as if it seemed more like a matter of life or death to him. Seeing Mrs. Gables now crouched down in front of the fireplace, throwing more coals in and stoking the fire up with a long metal fork, didn't help. She had placed enough coals to keep the fire burning for another month. In fact, it looked more like a bonfire. Maybe I was just reading too much into it? Maybe Mrs. Gables was just following orders? I continued to watch her as she stood up and stared at the fire, like she was making sure that it was just right. She seemed to be counting how many lumps of coal she had thrown into the burning flames. Maybe there was a correct amount to keep it fired up throughout the night? I guessed an old building like this – one without any central heating – would require a lot of coals, but to have to count them seemed way over the top. Just one more coal and I was sure that the bonfire would turn into an inferno. She seemed to be satisfied with the blaze as she turned away and walked toward us.

"Now, there are two rooms for you," she said, taking the lead and heading up the staircase. She was careful to keep her distance from us, always two stairs ahead, checking over her shoulder to make sure we weren't too close. Mrs. Gables pulled out a torch from her apron pocket and switched it on. "The electrics do not work upstairs, so we use torches."

Max, who was in front of me, turned and screwed up his face. "Torches? I thought Bishops were meant to be rich – surely he can afford to get them fixed?" he whispered.

"Not very romantic, is it?" said Jude, nudging me in the arm with his elbow. "Nothing like the passionate flames of candlelight."

"This isn't exactly a romantic setting now, is it?" I half-smiled. "A tatty, run-down old home fits torchlight perfectly." Maybe bishops weren't rich, after all he had just told us that the third floor was falling apart. A house this size must cost a fortune to keep maintained.

I looked over my shoulder to make sure that Raven was following. She glanced up at me with her black eyes, her face nearly drowned out with the approaching darkness as we reached the top of the stairs.

Mrs. Gables turned right and continued to walk down a hallway decorated with large paintings of portraits and scenic views. It was hard to tell what was on them, because as soon as the torchlight hit them, it soon left and moved on to the next painting. I turned around and looked back the way we had come. It was swallowed up with the dark and looked nothing more than a shadowy tunnel.

Taking another turn into a smaller hallway, Mrs. Gables stopped. "This is the first room." She pointed the torchlight at the door and then swung it round to another door opposite the first one. "And this is the other one." She took two keys from her pocket and unlocked each room. "The beds are made up and the fires are going. Be sure to keep them burning. I've left a pile of coals for each of you and that should be enough to keep it going throughout the night." She looked at us nervously, the light from the torch shinning up into her face made her head look too big for her body. "I've left a couple of nightdresses out for you two ladies and the bishop has kindly let you two use some of his old pyjamas." She turned to face Max and Jude, the torchlight now on them.

"That's nice," smiled Jude, trying not to laugh.

"That's very kind," said Max, ignoring Jude who stood and sniggered. "Could you tell me where the bathroom is please? Just in case one of us needs to use it during the night."

"There's no wandering about the hallways at night," whispered Mrs. Gables. "I've placed two bedpans under the beds just in case."

"*What*? I'm not using no bedpan," hissed Raven. "That's *disgusting*. We had better facilities at Cruor Pharma – at least we had a bathroom."

Ignoring Raven, Mrs. Gables backed away. "Breakfast is at 8. Stay in your rooms and don't forget the fires." She disappeared back down the hallway taking the torchlight with her. Her footsteps could be heard on the creaky floorboards as she retreated back the way we had come.

CHAPTER TWENTY TWO

I opened the door to the bedroom. The hallway was immediately lit up from the flames of one of Mrs. Gable's bonfires. The room was dusky and the floorboards bare, with only a small rug placed in the middle of the room. Two single beds were pushed up against the wall, a window between them. They had been made up with a single sheet and a crochet blanket covered the top. At the end of each bed I spotted a neatly folded nightdress, probably a couple of Mrs. Gables's, I should imagine. They looked like something you would wear back in the Victorian days. Wait until Raven spotted them – I could only begin to imagine what she would say. I smiled to myself.

"I don't like this room," hissed Raven, her face lit up in orangey-black shadows from the flames. "It's creepy."

"All old houses are creepy at night," whispered Max, plonking himself down on one of the beds. "At least we know we can get a good night's sleep without fear of demons and cleaners coming in."

"But do we know that for sure?" said Raven, lowering her voice, "What about ghosts? I bet there's plenty of them floating about."

"As long as they just float and don't attack me in my sleep, then I don't care," I whispered, pulling open the curtain and peering out into the dark. I shuddered. Our window overlooked the graveyard of St. Georges church. Not a view I really wanted after everything that had happened to us. Gravestones poked out from the ground like rows of broken, wonky teeth covered in the shadows of night. The rain had stopped falling but the wind was just as strong as it had been earlier when we'd first arrived at Dusk Fall Retreat. The large Ash trees still swayed frantically like arms of drowning people trying to stay afloat. I pulled the curtain shut as the glass rattled from a sudden strong gust of wind.

"Let's leave tomorrow," whispered Raven. "I don't like it here."

"Is there anywhere you *do* like?" asked Jude, pulling an old rocking chair across the floorboards and sitting down in it. The sound of the wooden rockers cut over the crackle and hiss of the flames, as Jude rocked slowly back and forth.

Raven shrugged her shoulders and didn't reply. She propped herself on the other bed leaning back against a pillow.

"Let's see how we all feel in the morning," I

yawned. "If everyone wants to leave tomorrow then I don't mind. Doctor Fletcher did say we needed to keep moving – not to stay in one place for too long."

"Fine with me," whispered Max. "I just want to find Robert."

"It's hard to know what the right thing to do is," said Jude. "We should be safe here from the cleaners but not from the police and Inspector Cropper. All they'd have to do is drag us out and hand us over to Middleton and the cleaners, but if we leave, then we can still get caught. If we go to Doctor Langstone then the chances are he will keep us for himself and he then gains control over the cleaners and their loyalty. We then lose ourselves forever and end up trapped within a demon-controlled body. We need to find somewhere that's safe to live – completely undetected or... we stay on the run – forever."

"Or we find a way to kill the demons," Max said. "There must be a way to get rid of them – surely?"

Raven sat up. "You can't kill demons. They have to be exorcized by a priest or bishop."

"What about us?" I whispered, perching on the end of the bed that Raven sat on. "If we kill the demons, then what happens to us?"

"What do you mean?" asked Jude, his blue eyes reflected with orange and yellow flashes from the fireplace.

"If we kill the demons, who's going to help us remove VA20 from our veins? If they die, do we die? We've got demon stuff in us – a part of them is now travelling through our veins – so does that mean, we die when they die?" I whispered, removing my boots and curling my legs up onto the bed.

No one answered. We sat in silence for a few minutes. Not one of us had an answer to my questions. We didn't know.

The fire continued to crackle and snap. The wind still rushed around outside. The silence was broken by a loud, dong... dong... dong... making us jump.

"It's just a clock," said Max. "I saw it down the hall – one of those old Grandfather clocks."

It continued to clang until it had let out twelve dongs. The house fell silent again.

"Midnight," whispered Jude, rocking slowly in his chair.

"The witching hour," hissed Raven. "When witches and ghosts appear to perform their unholy practices." She shuddered and looked toward the door. The hallway was black, like an abyss – silent as a grave.

"Shall we all sleep in here tonight?" Max whispered, his eyes trained on the open doorway. "I mean it's probably better if we stay together, right?"

"Max is feeling scared," sniggered Jude.

"I'm not scared... I just think that if anything did happen then we're stronger together... that's all," sighed Max. "Well, what do you think?"

"Come on then," smiled Jude, "let's go and get the pillows and blankets from the other room and we'll settle in here tonight."

"Throw some coals on the fire in there," I said, remembering the bishop's firm request to keep the fires burning.

"Why, what's the point if we're not sleeping in there tonight?" asked Jude, stopping at the doorway.

"The bishop seemed pretty pushy about keeping them burning all night – doesn't want to let the house get cold," I answered, walking over to the fireplace and scooping up some coals to throw in.

"Cold? This place is roasting with all these fires," said Jude. "Feels like I'm in a bloody sauna."

I shrugged my shoulders. "I know but that's what he wants and as we're his guests I think we should do as he asks."

"Okay, I'll do it," said Jude, following Max through the doorway.

I threw the coal onto the fire and turned to look at Raven. She was already asleep, sprawled out across the bed.

"Great," I whispered. "No room for me on the bed then."

Max and Jude returned with an armful of pillows and two blankets.

"Who's sleeping where?" asked Max, when he spotted Raven had fallen asleep and taken up one bed all to herself.

"Three in a bed," smiled Jude. "This could be interesting. As long as Kassidy's in the middle – no offence, Max."

"You can't fit three in that bed," I whispered. "One of us will have to sleep in the rocking chair."

"Or squeeze in next to Raven," said Max, looking at Jude.

"Don't look at me," said Jude. "I ain't sleeping next to her. She'll probably wake up in the middle of the night and kill me."

"Argue it out amongst yourselves," I smiled, jumping onto the empty bed. "I'm not sleeping next to her either, not after the way she was on

Ward 2." I shivered as I remembered last night, watching Raven from beneath the cover of my blanket, wondering if she was going to leap up and attack me – too scared to wake her after her crazy outbursts. I climbed under the crochet blanket and lay my head on the pillow. I was too tired to stay awake and see who I would be sharing the bed with. My eyes stung with tiredness and my head hurt. I could feel my eyelids drooping, closing. I was falling into stand-by mode – shutting down. I fell asleep.

CHAPTER TWENTY THREE

I lay, twisting and turning. I had no idea how long I had been asleep but my head felt fuzzy and my eyes heavy. It seemed that it had only been moments ago that I had got into this bed and shut my eyes. But it must have been longer as small snippets of a dream kept fluttering around inside my head. I turned over. The bed was uncomfortable. I plumped up the pillow and tried to relax. I wanted to go back to sleep but my mind was on overdrive, even though my body was begging for sleep.

I opened my eyes and sat up in bed, clutching the crochet blanket. The room was a mixture of dark shadows and dancing flames. My head felt dizzy and my eyelashes felt sticky – wet. I must have been crying in my sleep. What had I been dreaming of? I shook my head as I tried to remember. Memories of my dad seeped through my cloudy head as I started to recall parts of my dream. My dad had been standing in the creepy corridors of Cruor Pharma and Carly had been in it. I shuddered.

A noise in the room stirred me from my thoughts. I glanced from one dark corner to the next. My eyes fell upon the dark shape of the rocking chair by the end of my bed. I could just make out Max, his head poked out from beneath a blanket. I turned slightly in the bed and looked down beside me. Jude lay on his side, one arm draped over my lap. Shadows flickered across his bare chest, highlighting the muscles in his arms like a showpiece. The noise came again. What was it? It sounded like something falling – scattering to the floor. I looked over at Raven. She had her back to me, but she seemed to be sleeping peacefully. I tried to breathe calmly. Thoughts of Ward 2 seeped back into my head. I tried to push them away – reminding myself that I was no longer trapped there – I was in a place of safety now. I slowly slipped out from under Jude's arm. My bare feet recoiled at the cold floor and I rubbed them together to rid them of the chill that now threatened to travel up my legs. I shivered. I felt uneasy. The dream, or should I say nightmare, had left me feeling anxious – bothered. Braving the cold floor, I tiptoed over to the window and pulled the curtain aside. It was still dark. Nothing stirred outside. Even the wind had gone to sleep. The graveyard was void of life and for that I was grateful. I had half expected to see the floating dark shapes of the cleaners looming over the graves, waiting for us to leave the safety of the bishop's home. As my heart rate calmed the scattering noise came again. I spun around, my eyes wildly searching out the source from which it came from. I took a few steps forward. A loud thump from above startled me and I flinched down, fearful that something was going to fall on me. When nothing happened, I straightened up. I looked at Max. I wanted to wake him up. I didn't want to be the only one wandering around in the dark, half scared. I cocked my head to the side and strained my left ear – listening for movement above me. What could it have been? The bishop had said that the third floor was in disrepair, so what could be up there thumping around in the dead of night? I shook my head. I was just scaring myself. Max had been right in what he'd said about this house. All old houses were creepy, especially at night. They were like old men and women – full of aches and pains – creaks and groans.

I pulled up a wooden chair beside the fire. I was tired, yet restless. I wasn't ready to climb back into bed. My mind swam with too many thoughts – dark thoughts – horrendous images kept replaying over and over again like I was being forced to watch them – brainwashed. I was sure that if they carried on being replayed, I would eventually turn insane. Was that what had happened to Sylvia Green? Why she was now locked up in a mental institute? Had she gone crazy with horrendous images constantly playing in her head? Or had she become dangerous like Howard and Wendy? And what of Robert and Alex? We knew nothing about their state of health or mind, only of what the bishop had told us, and that hadn't really been much. It was hard to compare Max, Raven, Jude, and myself to Robert, Alex and Sylvia; after all, they had been given a different batch – a different strain of this demon stuff – theirs being VA10 and ours VA20. I wondered if that was the reason Ben Fletcher had said I was Doctor Middleton's breakthrough miracle. VA10 obviously hadn't worked the way that Middleton had wanted it to. Did that mean that VA20 wouldn't kill me? My body had withstood the drug so far. I hadn't turned into one of those zombie-creatures. I pulled up the sleeve of my top and looked at the black veins. If I could stay one step ahead of the cleaners and avoid all lone demons then maybe I stood a chance? Maybe I could live with VA20 inside me? That glimmer of hope was soon squashed when my mind started to unravel it. VA20 still hadn't worked its way all around my body yet. It could still kill me when it had filled every single vein in me. What would I become?

I shovelled up some more coals with the brass scoop and threw them onto the fire. It crackled and hissed, sending seething hot sparks up the chimney. My mind started to wander back to Hannah. I screwed my eyes shut, willing the image of her jumping from the balcony away. I didn't want to watch it again. I wanted to change the channel – watch a different programme. Music videos or a comedy would do. *The Office* or *Friends* always made me laugh. If only I had a remote control or the buttons to switch over the horror that kept haunting my head. I stood up and paced back and forth. Why couldn't I rid myself of these awful images that were screwing up my head? Why wouldn't my brain just shut down and give me some peace? I could feel myself filling with anger – frustration. I just wanted to sleep. I wanted to escape my own mind and sleep was the only place I could forget. I kicked out at the chair. It toppled over – clattering onto the bare floorboards. I didn't care if I woke the others. Why should they sleep so peacefully? I was fired up. Ready for a fight. I wanted to hit someone – anyone. I wanted to vent my anger. Make them feel the pain that I was suffering – hurt them like I was hurting – spill their blood like mine had. I grabbed large clumps of my hair in both fists and yanked down hard, gritting my teeth. I wanted to scream at the top of my voice – yell so hard – go on some mad frenzy – smashing everything up that I came across. I wanted everyone to feel my pain.

"I just want some *fucking sleep*," I snapped through my gritted teeth. Tears spilled down over my face.

"Hey, come here," a voice whispered through the dark.

I spun around. My tears of anger turned into tears of sadness. I stood and faced Jude. He was standing at the end of the bed in just his trousers, his hair messed up. He held out his hand for me to take.

I swallowed down the hard lump stuck in my throat – my breathing a series of short judders. I took a step nearer and tried to wipe my frustrated tears away, but they kept coming.

"I'm messed up... I can't stop thinking about everything," I sniffed, "I just want to sleep. I want to wake up and go back to my life before I lost my job – before I lost my dad. I'd rather spend the rest of my life watching him get pissed every night than live through all this *shit*... all this death... blood... hell. I don't want to be here... I don't want this." I looked down at my feet. My tears splashed them.

"I want someone to take me away from all this… I want to get off this awful ride but it won't stop – it keeps getting faster. I'm stuck, I can't get out." I threw my hands up to my face and covered my eyes.

"Hey, I've got you, I'll keep you safe, we'll get off this ride… I promise." Jude wrapped his arms around me.

The warmth from his body comforted me – soothed me – wrapped me in a cocoon. I hugged my arms around him and held him tight. I needed this. I wanted to feel safe. I wanted to feel company. I wanted to rid myself of this loneliness that engulfed me.

"Look at me," hushed Jude, taking my chin in his hand and tilting my head up. "I won't let anyone take you. I'll look after you – all of you – even Raven – okay?"

I stared into his eyes. They were so crystal clear it was like looking into eternity. For the little time I had known Jude, this was the first time I had seen him look so sincere – so heartfelt. I wanted to believe him – I wanted to believe he could keep us all safe. I had to. I didn't know if I had it in me to keep going – to stay strong – to stay safe – to remain sane.

"I'll make you feel better," whispered Jude,

wiping an escaped tear away from my cheek.
"Come on." He took my hand and led me back to
the bed. I climbed under the covers and let Jude
hold me close. His warm, smooth skin against me
eased the troubles that were fighting inside my
head – calmed me like I was floating on a velvety
still ocean. I looked up into his eyes. That alluring
twinkle seemed to send a message to me – a
message telling me to kiss him. I looked down at
his lips. They almost begged me to taste them. I
wanted more than a hug to make me feel better. I
wanted Jude. I wanted his body to wrap itself
around mine and overpower me. I closed my eyes
and felt his lips against mine. But it wasn't enough.
I pulled him against me – my hands slipped over his
tight skin – my fingers roamed over the muscles of
his stomach. My body ached for him – craved for
more than just his touch. His hands slipped under
my top – his fingers releasing the catch on my bra.
Before I knew it, my top was off and I could feel his
skin pressed against my breasts. He pushed me
down on the bed and climbed over me. His lips
floated over the skin of my neck and down
between my breasts. I reached down and gently
eased his face back up to mine. He kissed my lips
and whispered softly into my ear.

"I wanted you the moment I saw you."

I opened my eyes. What the hell was I doing? Was I losing it? I looked down at my naked chest covered in a criss-cross of black veins and then back up into Jude's face. I couldn't do this. Not now. I had needed company, craved for someone to show me some love, but this was just going to open up a can of worms that I really didn't need right now. I had enough problems without adding a guy to the list. I pushed Jude away and sat up.

"I'm sorry," I whispered. "I can't do this. I'm not thinking straight." I gathered up my top and covered my chest, suddenly feeling uncomfortable. What had I been thinking? Getting involved like that with Jude was a recipe for disaster. Not to mention that there were two other people in the room with us. I shook my head like I was trying to put some sense into me.

"It's okay," whispered Jude, his eyes looked sad – disappointed. "Maybe it is too soon? Maybe another time?"

I felt bad – guilty. I hadn't meant to lead him on. I looked down at the floor in shame. "Let's just get some sleep." I turned my back on him and pulled on my top.

"How about a cuddle then?" whispered Jude, lying back down on the bed beside me.

I nodded my head. That was the least I could offer after leading him up the garden path and then dumping him. I lay down and let Jude wrap his arms about me. Willing myself to fall asleep, I closed my eyes tight.

CHAPTER TWENTY FOUR

The sun trickled through the gaps in the curtain making beams of light shine across the bedroom. The fire still burnt in the hearth but had died down a little through the night. I could hear the distant sounds of bird calls coming from outside. I sat perched on my elbows feeling somewhat relieved that we were all still here – we had made it through the night. I looked down at Jude. He was fast asleep. I felt my cheeks flush as I remembered what had happened between us during the night. I felt stupid now – almost giving myself away like that. I hoped that everything would be all right between us when he woke up. Would he be angry? Would he be hoping that there was something between us now? That we would be more than just friends? Did I want more than that? I really wasn't sure.

"What an idiot I am," I mumbled. I really needed to get a grip. If the others could hold it together without jumping on each other's bodies then I should also. I took a deep breath – even though I had messed up last night, I felt stronger somehow. Maybe the few hours I had managed to sleep had helped me. Maybe the sun shining through the window had brightened my spirits and left me feeling ready and hopeful for the future. Or perhaps it was because I felt more trusting of Jude. He had showed me a more caring side to him last night even though we had almost ended up sleeping with each other. I felt that I could trust him and that gave me some comfort. The worrying feelings I had felt yesterday on discovering the unplugged iPod at Hannah's flat – the scary thoughts I had worried about – if I could trust the others, seemed to be a long way away now. I still didn't have an answer as to how the iPod had been unplugged, but we had travelled together this far and had helped each other when we had needed to. Surely that meant something. If one of us was out to get the others, I'm sure it would have happened already.

I looked over at Max. Somehow he had managed to sleep all through the night on that wooden rocking chair. His blonde hair lay in silky strands across his face. He looked deep in sleep. I watched as his bare chest rose and fell with each dreamful breath he took. The black veins stood out like a sore thumb against his pale skin but hadn't seemed to spread any further. That was a good sign. I wondered if I had fared the same during the night.

I slipped out from Jude's arms and pulled on my boots. I needed the bathroom and I sure as hell wasn't going to use the bedpan that Mrs. Gables had placed under the bed. A loud snore came from Raven and I smiled to myself. Hopefully a good night's sleep had done wonders for her grumpy moods. I tiptoed across the bedroom and opened the door.

Not really knowing which way I should head, I decided to go along the hallway and check each door until I came across the bathroom. The first two doors were locked so I carried on until I came to the end. A small window allowed the sunlight through and I took a moment to gaze out onto the sunny morning. The window looked over the back garden. It was mainly lawn with a few shrubs and more Ash trees. Some stepping stones led up the garden to where a birdbath had been placed next to a set of garden chairs and table. Beyond the garden lay rolling fields of purple lavender and fields of wheat. I opened the window and breathed in the cool autumn morning. It reminded me of happier times. Days out in the country with Hannah and her parents. I stood for a while just staring out – wanting to hold on to those happy memories – if only I could pull them all in and place those memories in a glass jar – keep them forever – take one out when I was having a bad day and relive it again.

As I gazed out across the fields, Mrs. Gables came into sight. She was walking down the garden, carrying a basketful of wet washing. She stopped and started to hang up the clothes, carefully placing each item over the washing line and fixing them down with pegs. By the time she had finished, the washing line was full of the bishop's shirts and trousers. A couple of Mrs. Gable's flowery dresses had made it onto the line also, and as I went to walk away, something caught my eye. An odd piece of clothing had been hung onto the end of the line. It was a T-shirt with a picture of Beyoncé on it. Why would Mrs. Gables or the bishop have such an item of clothing? I couldn't imagine either of them wearing it. I couldn't imagine either of them being a fan of Beyoncé's music. I tried to picture in my head what the bishop would look like wearing it with his long overgrown beard and eyebrows. What kind of event would he go to dressed in it? It certainly wasn't something for church sermons – no, it couldn't be his – but that only left Mrs. Gables. I sniggered to myself as I imagined her wearing it to a music concert – her apron tied over it – dancing along to *Drunk in Love*. Smiling, I walked back along the hallway. Everyone has their secret passion, their favourite tipple or treat – what was the harm? As long as they weren't hurting anyone – who was I to mock Mrs. Gables and her love of Beyoncé? I turned into the corridor which ran above the main hallway. Looking down I could see that Mrs. Gables was still keeping her bonfire burning. The morning was warm and sunny; why keep the fire going? I guessed they were both stuck in their old ways – a bit eccentric.

I tried a couple more doors and finally came to the bathroom. Closing the door behind me, I used the toilet and then went to the sink and filled it up with warm water. A clean flannel had been placed beside the sink along with a bar of Pears soap. A quick wash would do. After the shower incident at Hannah's flat, I had no intention of stepping foot inside one of them again. Taking a quick look around the bathroom, I soon realised that there was no shower, just an old roll-top bath. Looking at the chipped tiles around the wall, it was obvious that the bathroom hadn't been modernised for a very long time.

I took my top off so I could have a look at myself in the mirror. I wanted to see how many more black veins had appeared overnight. It had been too dark last night when Jude had pulled my top off to see if they had got any worse. I was relieved to see that nothing much had changed – the VA20 hadn't really spread. It was probably clogging up and getting stuck. I wasn't sure if that was a good thing or not. Slowing the spread could bide me more time, but then if my veins were clogging up then that wasn't good. Father Williams's Rosary beads still hung around my neck. I took hold of the cross and gave it a little tug. I wanted to make sure it was going to stay put. I didn't want to lose it. Even if it didn't work on demons, at least it would help me against the cleaners.

I cleaned my face and then leant over the bath and washed my hair. After I had towel-dried it, I pulled my top back on and left the bathroom.

I was about to head back to the bedroom and wake the others when I noticed another set of small staircases at the end of the corridor. One led down to the lower floor, and the other up to the third floor. I stood at the bottom of the stairs and looked up, remembering the loud thump I had heard last night. Curious to see what the state of the third floor looked like, I took a couple of steps up and stopped – not too sure as to whether I should risk going up there after we had been told not to. I didn't want to get caught by Mrs. Gables or the bishop. But then who would see me if even they didn't go up there? My feet naturally took another few steps up like they had a mind of their own, and before I knew it, I was almost at the top. I stopped and re-questioned whether or not I should carry on. *Perhaps I shouldn't,* I tried to tell myself. I didn't want to go falling through the floor and end up landing on the bishop while he lay asleep in his bed – that wouldn't be good. But perhaps just a tiny peek wouldn't hurt. I carried on. After reaching the top, I was disappointed to see that the third floor was shut off by a padlocked door. It was bolted over by several locks. I shook my head. Why tell us not to go up here when we couldn't get in anyway? As I turned to leave, the creak of the floorboards down below filtered up and I froze.

"Shit," I cursed under my breath. Was that the bishop or Mrs. Gables? It didn't matter which one it was – both would be angry if they caught me up here. I crouched down low against the padlocked door and hoped that whoever it was wouldn't come up here. As I waited for the floorboards to stop creaking down below, I noticed what looked like five black smudged fingerprints at the bottom of the door. How strange. Why would anyone try to open the door from the bottom? Maybe it had become stuck once and the bishop or Mrs. Gables had tried to pry it open from that angle? I quickly checked the rest of the door for further fingerprints but there were no more.

Peering down the staircase, I listened quietly to see if I could hear any more movement from down below. Silence. It was as still as the dead of night. Whoever it had been had gone, or at least I hoped they had. I didn't want to be trapped up here for ages. Taking a few steps at a time, I quietly made my way back down the stairs. The corridor was empty and I hastily headed back to the bedroom.

CHAPTER TWENTY FIVE

I was pleased to see that Jude, Max, and Raven had woken up.

"How are you this morning?" asked Jude, smiling at me. "Feel better?"

I nodded my head and felt my cheeks go red. "Yes, a lot better…. thanks for putting up with me…" I didn't know what to say. I felt awkward. "Sorry I woke you up."

"No probs," he smiled, pulling on his shirt and buttoning it up. "I'm always here to help a damsel in distress." He winked at me.

At least he didn't seem angry, I thought. That was a relief. I could live with the embarrassment more than having to put up with him being pissed at me.

"You had a bad night?" said Max, holding his black leather jacket over his shoulder.

"Yes, but I'm fine now," I said, picking up the satchel and just wanting to get off the subject. "In fact, I feel great – ready to take on any shit that falls at my feet."

"Are we gonna leave now?" mumbled Raven. She still wore the leather jacket I had given her yesterday, she had slept in it all night.

"Breakfast first," said Jude, "I'm starving."

"When aren't you?" smiled Max. He turned to look at me. "Do you think the bishop has a top I could have? I can't go around with a bare chest forever and I can't live in this jacket all day and every day."

"Fancy yourself in a dog's collar, do you?" smiled Jude.

"Not really what I was thinking of," said Max, heading for the bedroom door. "A shirt or jumper would do."

"Mrs. Gables might be able to help you out there," I smiled, remembering the Beyoncé T-shirt I had seen hanging on the washing line.

"I'd rather have the dog's collar than one of Mrs. Gable's flowery dresses, thanks, Kassidy." Max opened the door.

"Come on then," I said, pushing past Max and heading out into the hallway. "Let's go and have breakfast and see if we can get you a top to wear."

The smell of bacon and toast wafted up the stairs as we headed down into the large hall. My stomach rumbled, even though I had eaten well the night before.

Jude strolled into the dining room and we followed close behind. The table had been set for breakfast and the small fire still burned away in the hearth. We took our seats, eager to tuck in.

Mrs. Gables appeared at the door carrying a tray with dishes covered with silver lids. As soon as she saw us sat at the table she almost flinched and hesitated, obviously contemplating on changing her mind and leaving the room now that we were there.

"Morning, Mrs. Gables," I said, wanting to engage her in some kind of conversation. I didn't want to let her off the hook – let her vanish – avoid us. "Breakfast smells good."

She nodded her head as she placed the dishes down, but still didn't speak. I wanted her to see that we were normal human beings – not monsters. It bothered me to think that anyone would try to avoid us just because we had these unsightly black veins and twisted nails. Looks weren't everything, and although I knew that we must look weird, underneath we were all safe – we still had feelings. I would have understood her fear about us if we had climbed out from one of the graves in St. George's church, but she knew we had come from Cruor Pharma and the way we looked wasn't our fault. Surely she felt a little more comfortable around us now that we had spent a night here. We hadn't climbed from our beds and tried to kill her, and neither had Robert, Alex, and Sylvia when they had stayed here.

"Is the bishop having breakfast with us?" I asked, still trying to get a word out of her.

She shook her head and turned to leave.

I stood up, frustrated that she wouldn't even look at me. "Mrs. Gables, I know you must think of us like we have the plague or something but we don't mean you any harm. It's not catching and you won't wake up in the morning looking like us. We're just four people who needed a place to stay and some answers – that's all."

"Well said," mumbled Jude over a mouthful of bacon. "I guess we're crowding your holy space and there's no room for people who have had the misfortune of dancing with the devil and his followers. But fear no more, Mrs. Gables, we will be on our way soon and then you will never have to look upon our demon-like bodies again – you can turn back to your Bible and thank your God that we will no longer cross your holy path." Jude turned to look up at Mrs. Gables, a sarcastic smile across his face.

The room fell silent. An uncomfortable atmosphere lingered on the air. I watched Mrs. Gables as she dithered by the door, unsure as to whether she should leave or face us.

"It has nothing to do with my religion." She spoke with a sharp tongue, which took me by surprise. She had seemed so meek and timid that she was the last person I would have suspected to speak with such a harshness to her voice.

"What is it then?" asked Max, causally leaning back in his seat. Max, who seemed normally chilled and wouldn't hurt a fly, even had a look of annoyance over his face. His happy green eyes looked pissed. An irritation lingered behind them. "Why don't you like us being here?"

"I wish you'd never turned up here at the bishop's," snapped Mrs. Gables, her lips screwed up and her eyes narrowed. "Do you have any idea what an inconvenience you all are being here? What a difficult situation you've put myself and the bishop in?"

"No, please tell us," smiled Jude his voice – cocky.

"We've had people like *you* here before," Mrs. Gables spat, smacking her fists down onto the table. "Life was good, life was peaceful, and then those freaks turned up and upset everything. Now I've got you four to deal with."

Raven stood up and slammed her fists down, her face just inches from Mrs. Gables. "I'm sorry," Raven peered into Mrs, Gables's eyes.

"We'll just go back to Cruor Pharma and ask if they'll be kind enough to remove this *demon-shit* from our veins and then I'll go to church and beg the Lord for forgiveness for asking to be injected with this crap and for inconveniencing your perfect *holy life*. After all, we asked for this, didn't we?" Raven looked round at us. "We all volunteered to be turned into people-eating, crazy-killing freaks that rip people apart and eat their intestines! We want to fuck people up and kill them – it's fun... maybe you should book yourself an appointment with Doctor Middleton, after all, you can see how much we love looking like this."

Raven sat down. Even after a good night's sleep she still looked like something that had been dragged out from the gutter – her face sullen and cloudy, her black hair back to looking greasy and stringy. Mrs. Gables certainly hadn't done anything for Raven's mood.

"I don't want any of you here," Mrs. Gables continued. "If you go, then you might speak out about me and the bishop and then we'll end up with the same fate as Father Peter or Father William. If you stay then you'll change like..."

The door to the dining room suddenly opened and the bishop walked in.

"Good morning, everyone," he smiled.

"Sorry I'm late for breakfast but I had to take the morning service. Sometimes I wonder why I still bother. The congregation has fallen to such a small number that I wonder whether it's worth heating the church these days and instruct the parishioners to attend the Sacred Heart in Rane. Anyway, they are my problems to sort out. I trust Mrs. Gables is looking after you all?"

We sat in silence and looked at each other, unsure as to whether the bishop had heard our raised voices. We waited to see if Mrs. Gables would continue her rant. But she just stood looking somewhat deflated – back to her usual meek, timid demeanour.

"I've been looking after them just fine." She smiled awkwardly. "Would you like some black pudding, my dear?" She held out the bowl toward Raven, a forced kindness in her voice. "It's very good."

Raven recoiled back in her seat, a look of revulsion across her face.

"I don't eat blood," she hissed, screwing her nose up. "It's disgusting – the fluid of evil." She poked around the food on her plate, picking it up with her fork and inspecting it closely. She obviously still believed that Mrs. Gables was lacing the food with poison – and who could blame her

225

after the angry outburst that had just happened?

"Help yourselves," said the bishop, pouring himself a cup of fresh tea and ignoring Raven. "I hope you all slept well?"

"Yes, thank you," smiled Max, watching Mrs. Gables leave the room. He had put on his jacket again – probably too embarrassed to sit bare-chested.

"We were wondering if you had a spare shirt or jumper that Max could wear. He only has that jacket, you see," I asked, piling my plate with bacon, sausages, and black pudding.

The bishop sat quiet for a few moments and then said, "I think I have a T-shirt you could use. I'll ask Mrs. Gables to find you one."

"Thank you," smiled Max, taking a sip of his coffee.

The very mention of her name seemed to quieten us all. Now I knew what her problem was it made leaving here easier. There was no way I wanted to stay another night in a house where I wasn't welcome. Even though the bishop had been kind, I still felt uncomfortable being around someone who obviously hated the very sight of us. I had been wrong in believing that Mrs. Gables was scared of us. Instead she was one of those people who wanted to turn a blind eye to any kind of trouble – bury her head in the sand and rid herself of anything that could cause her problems. It made me feel sad, but didn't really surprise me. Would I want the likes of the cleaners, the doctors, or the bent police disposing of me because I knew too much? Probably not, but I would like to think that if that situation had arisen that I wouldn't turn my back on someone who needed my help. I guessed that the bishop had no idea how Mrs. Gables really felt. He seemed quite oblivious to her behaviour around us. At least he was a kind soul. But what I couldn't tell was whether Mrs. Gables wanted us to leave or stay. She seemed annoyed by either option. But that was the only two outcomes – unless she had plans to dispose of us – bump us off and hide our bodies. I shivered.

I looked over at Jude. He was still stuffing his chops. I smiled at him when he looked up at me. His cocky speech to Mrs. Gables had left her silent for a few moments and I felt my lips turn up into a small grin. Even Raven had stuck it to Mrs. Gables. It actually felt good to be a part of this group. The more time I spent with Jude, Max, and Raven, the more I felt comfortable with them. We all had a horrible secret that we shared but I was glad to see that we would all get stuck in and watch over each other.

Pushing his plate away, Max looked at the bishop. "Did Robert and the other two leave on foot or did they have a car?"

"They left on foot," said the bishop, eyeing Raven with a wary look as she sniffed at a slice of bacon. "I did try to stop them, but Robert wouldn't listen. He was determined to get to Doctor Langstone's. I had no choice but to let them leave – I couldn't force them to stay."

"Did you know that Sylvia tried to kill herself?" I asked, stirring a spoonful of sugar into my tea. "She tried to jump off a bridge."

The bishop sat and shook his head. "No, I didn't know that. If only they had stayed here. Is that what you meant last night when you said that Sylvia hadn't made it? Is she dead?"

"No, she's been locked up in a mental institute," I answered. "We don't know if it's because of the drug she was given – if it turned her crazy – or whether she was so disturbed that she couldn't go on and tried to kill herself."

"Or maybe it's something else," Jude suddenly piped in. He stared intently at the bishop. "Maybe what happened to your Father Peter is what almost happened to Sylvia."

"You think that something from Cruor Pharma caught up with Sylvia and tried to deal with her before she could speak out against Doctor Middleton?" said Max, finishing his cup of coffee.

Jude shrugged his shoulders. "Who knows? Anything is possible."

"It would make sense for Middleton to erase anyone who might speak out against him. We know he's got the police covering up for him, but Sylvia and your brother and Alex got past them, so he probably sent out the cleaners like he's done for us." I pushed my plate away and sat back in my seat. "Only they didn't get to finish off the job – Sylvia is still alive."

The bishop looked worried. I could see it in his eyes – that unmistakable look of fear cowered underneath his bushy eyebrows. He sat silent for a few minutes and then stood up. Using both hands to lean against the table he peered at us.

"Now, have you all had a good think about staying here with me and Mrs. Gables? There's plenty of room and you can all stay safely inside without fear of being seen."

"We're leaving," hissed Raven. "I'm not staying locked up in here where you can't use the toilet at night and the housekeeper wants you dead." She stood up, her hands firmly placed on her hips.

The bishop looked rather taken aback by

her outburst. "I'm sure we can come to some arrangements to make you all feel at home. Mrs. Gables is trying her best to make you all feel comfortable – there isn't one harmful bone in her body. It's not safe for you all to leave. Now that you're here, I really think it would be in our best interests if you stay put."

"Thank you for being so concerned about us," I said, trying to smooth over the bad feeling that was now evident in the room thanks to Raven. I looked over at her and glared. Why couldn't she pick the right moments to open her mouth? Mrs. Gables deserved what Raven had said to her, but the bishop hadn't. Why did she have to be so rude all the time? Raven needed to learn when it was okay to speak out and when it wasn't. "We really can't stay. We have to find Robert and we need to see Doctor Langstone."

"We really appreciate you taking us in last night," said Max. "You have helped us more than you know. If it wasn't for my brother then maybe I'd stay, but I can't."

The bishop let out a heavy sigh and nodded his head. "I see I'm not going to persuade you... but before you leave... let me get Mrs. Gables to find you that top you wanted."

He walked over to the cord that made the

bell chime and tugged on it. Within a couple of minutes, Mrs. Gables appeared, her eyes avoiding our stare.

"Could you find Max a T-shirt to wear? I'm sure we have a spare one that he could use," asked the bishop.

"I'll go and fetch one," said Mrs. Gables, eyeing us nervously again. She backed out of the doorway. I was sure she thought we were going to pounce on her and infect her. Why bother to keep up the pretence? We had made it perfectly clear that we weren't infected with something that she could catch. I guess she wanted to keep up her timid, whiter-than white appearance to the bishop. Mrs. Gables – the faithful Christian who would do anything for the bishop.

"Now, promise me you will come back here if you come into any trouble," said the bishop, trying to smooth over his bushy beard. "My door is always open."

"We will, thanks," said Jude, standing up.

Mrs. Gables appeared back at the dining room door. She held out a grey T-shirt for Max to take.

"Thanks," said Max, eyeing Mrs. Gables with a wary look. "I'll just pop upstairs and put this on."

We left the dining room and waited in the large hall for Max. The fire was still burning bright and the bishop threw on some more coals. Although I had woken feeling hopeful, now as we waited to leave, I couldn't help but feel nervous. We were going back out there into the unknown. What would we find? I walked over to a small window and peered out onto the gravel driveway. The morning was bright and the sun still shone. Nothing seemed out of place. Just an ordinary autumn day to most people, but to us it was more than that. It wasn't just a dark day that produced shadows and monsters. Demons could still hide in the sun.

CHAPTER TWENTY SIX

Max appeared at the top of the staircase. He walked down holding the leather jacket in his hand. I felt my mouth drop open as I saw the picture on his T-shirt. It had the face of Pinhead on it from the film *Hellraiser*. The words printed over it read *He'll tear your soul apart*. I looked at the bishop and tried to picture him wearing it. I shook my head. There was no way it could be his.

"Nice top," smiled Jude, nodding his head in approval.

Raven stomped her foot on the floor and tutted, "Why does everyone else get to wear all the good stuff? It's not fair – I've got flowers on a blouse and bows on my shoes."

Ignoring Jude and Raven admiring the T-shirt, I looked at the bishop. I couldn't help but ask. "Is that your T-shirt?"

The bishop nodded his head. "Yes, it is, and Max is more than welcome to wear it."

"You really like the Hellraiser films?" I asked, still finding it hard to believe.

"The what?" asked the bishop?

"Hellraiser... you like Pinhead?" I said, pointing out the T-shirt on Max.

As if seeing the T-shirt for the first time, the bishop took a few steps forward and peered at the picture on the front. "He'll tear your... soul apart? Goodness me, whatever is that? I've never seen this top before, of course it isn't mine." The bishop screwed up his nose as if disgusted by the T-shirt.

"Well... whose is it?" I asked, raising an eyebrow.

"Urmmm... it must belong to Mrs. Gables. Yes, I think I've seen her using it as a duster," said the bishop. "That's right, she picked it up at the church fete last year. It had been left behind."

"Really?" I smiled and looked away. I wanted to ask who was the Beyoncé fan but thought better of it. I didn't want to annoy the bishop. He had been kind to us after all.

"Well, I guess we'd better get going," said Max. "Thanks again and thank you for taking my brother in, you gave him a roof over his head when he most needed it. I really do appreciate your help."

"Just let me know of any news you hear about Robert, and please take care of yourself – all of you." The bishop smiled and unlocked the front door.

We stepped out into the sunshine. The tall Ash trees rustled in the light breeze and the distant sound of a cockerel could be heard. Waving goodbye to the bishop, our feet crunched over the gravel as we headed for Jude's car. I was relieved that Mrs. Gables hadn't come to the door to say goodbye. I didn't care to see her again. As far as I was concerned, she wasn't a true member of the church – just someone who took the parts of being religious that suited her – part time – a pretender. She liked the image but that was as far as it went.

Jude opened up the boot and I placed the satchel inside along with the leather jacket that Max had been wearing. I was about to shut it when I heard Jude swear.

"What the fuck? Look at this."

I joined the others at the front of the car.

"What's wrong?" I asked, looking at Jude's angry face.

"My tyres, that's what's wrong," he moaned. "How are we gonna leave now?"

I crouched down. Both front tyres were as flat as pancakes.

"How the hell did that happen?" I said shaking my head. "They were fine yesterday when you drove the car up onto the driveway."

"Looks like someone's let them down," said Max. "They couldn't have both got punctures at the same time."

Raven looked around as if expecting to see the culprit jump out from one of the shrubs. "Mrs. Gables did it," she hissed. "Her poisoned food didn't work on us and now she wants us back to finish the job."

We looked at each other as if silently considering what Raven had just said could be possible. We all knew now how Mrs. Gables felt about us but would she really come out here and let down Jude's tyres? I knew she wasn't happy about us being here, so I wouldn't think that she would try to stop us from going. But we also knew that she didn't want us leaving and mentioning her or the bishop to anyone who would bring trouble back to Dusk Fall Retreat. I turned back to face the old house with its tall, looming chimney stacks. My stomach somersaulted when I spotted Mrs. Gables peering out from one of the bedroom windows at us. She turned away when she saw me staring up at her. I looked over at Raven. Maybe she was right. Maybe Mrs. Gables was out to finish us off.

CHAPTER TWENTY SEVEN

"We'll walk," said Raven, her face dark and gloomy.

"Walk?!" said Max. "Do you have any idea how long that will take us to reach Derbyshire?"

Raven shrugged her shoulders. "I don't care, as long as we don't have to stay here again." She looked back at the bishop's house and shivered.

"We need to pump up the tyres and then get on our way," said Jude. "We can't walk. It's not just the distance that's the problem. We stand more of a chance if we go by car. On foot, we'll stand out like a sore thumb. Any police cars that happen to go by while we're all trekking to Derby will check us out – especially as they're looking for us."

I stood up. I had been checking over the tyres and the news wasn't good. "The tyres weren't let down," I said. "They've been slashed."

"What?" Jude bent down and closely inspected his wheels. "Shit, you're right."

"So now we know for sure that this was deliberate. That kind of changes everything," I said. "Who do you think did it?"

"The cleaners," hissed Raven, coming to stand closer to us.

"No way," said Max. "This isn't something they would do, this isn't their way. They wouldn't bother playing silly games like this. They're demons – they don't need to do this. And if they were here, don't you think they would have got us by now? We've been standing outside for the last ten minutes – they don't hang back and wait for the right moment. You heard what Doctor Fletcher said to Kassidy. They're relentless – one mistake made by us and they'll take you, me, Jude, and Kassidy."

"Well it couldn't have been the police," said Jude. "If they knew we were here then they would have just come into the house and arrested us."

"I guess that leaves Mrs. Gables," I whispered, removing the satchel from the boot of the car.

"Even more reason to just leave and go on foot," pushed Raven. "They're gonna kill us."

"Don't be so fucking stupid," said Jude. "Kill us? They could have done that last night when we were all asleep. Why bother slashing the tyres and getting us to stay another night? He's a bishop for fuck's sake, he preaches from the Bible. He doesn't wander around with a kitchen knife slashing tyres and killing his guests – this isn't a scene from

Psycho and the bishop isn't Norman Bates."

I looked back up at the window where I had seen Mrs. Gables watching us. It must have been her who had damaged the tyres. I was with Jude on this one. I couldn't believe that the bishop meant us any harm. He had seemed genuinely concerned about Robert and had shown us nothing but kindness by letting us stay the night. I could only assume that Mrs. Gables wanted to keep us here through fear that her and the bishop would come under Doctor Middleton's radar if we left and spoke about them. Still, it did make me feel uneasy. I was sure that Mrs. Gables wasn't the type to harm us. After all, Robert, Alex, and Sylvia had left here unharmed. We knew that for sure as Sylvia was now in a mental institute, and if Mrs. Gables was the murdering type, she wouldn't have let the others leave. But it did make me feel a little on edge.

"What are we going to do then?" I asked. "We don't really have many good options – if any."

Max lent against the car and ran his fingers through his long blonde hair. "We go back to the bishop and ask if there's anywhere nearby where we can replace the tyres."

"How are we gonna pay for them? Tyres aren't cheap and we only have £80 left," I reminded him.

"We'll ask the bishop for the money," said Jude, closing the car door and locking it. "I'm sure he'll help us out."

"A bishop who uses torchlight at night isn't gonna have the money to give us for tyres," hissed Raven. "We're wasting time. We should just go now and find Robert and Alex."

"Hey, I want to find my brother more than anything but walking is dumb," said Max, heading back toward the house. "If we can get the tyres fixed then it's worth a short delay."

"The longer we stay here, the more chance we give the cleaners of catching up with us," moaned Raven, reluctantly following behind Max.

"I know," said Max. "But it's a chance we'll have to take."

As we reached the front door, it was suddenly swung open. The bishop stood just inside, a look of bewilderment across his face.

"I wasn't expecting to see you all so soon," he smiled. "Have you changed your minds about staying?"

"No," glared Raven. "Some freak has knifed up our tyres."

"My goodness," tutted the bishop. "We've never had a problem with crime here before. The village has always been a safe, friendly neighbourhood to live in. Who would have done such a thing?"

Before Raven could open her mouth and accuse the bishop or Mrs. Gables, I stepped in. "We don't know, but we need to get two new tyres and we don't have enough money to pay for them. Is there any chance we could borrow some money from you? I know you've already helped us out by giving us a bed for the night, but if we don't get new tyres then we're stuck." I looked at the bishop with pleading eyes.

"The money isn't the problem," the bishop said, stepping aside and letting us back into the large hall. "I'm afraid you won't find anywhere open today – it is Sunday after all. Everywhere around here is shut."

Sunday - I had lost track of time. With everything that had happened to me I had completely forgotten the day of the week. Now what were we gonna do?

"Are you sure there's no garages open nearby?" asked Jude. "Or someone in the village that might be able to help us out?"

The bishop closed the door behind us and turned the key. Then bending down, he slid the bolt closed and then slid the one at the top of the door. He must have seen the confusion in our faces at him locking up so early on in the day as he said, "Better to be safe than sorry – if there's someone about committing crime then we don't want them getting in here and doing goodness knows what."

"Is there someone in the village who could help us?" Jude asked again.

"I wouldn't think so," answered the bishop, placing the key inside his pocket. "Most of the locals rarely leave the village. There isn't much need for having a car here."

"But they must have to go out and do their shopping," I said. "They can't all live like hermit crabs here."

"Most of the locals are elderly, they have shopping brought to them," smiled the bishop as he ushered us into the snug. "I'm afraid you won't find any help here today, but there is a bus that runs along the main road just outside the village. You could catch that tomorrow morning at 10:30 and go into the small town of Rane. There's a garage there and I'm sure you will be able to get your tyres sorted."

"A bus – 10:30?!" hissed Raven. "That's no good, we need to go now – today." She glared at the bishop and then flung herself down onto one of the sofas like a child having a tantrum.

242

"I'm very sorry, but it looks like you will have to spend another night here," the bishop said, combing his fingers through his beard.

A scattering noise came from the chimney and made me jump. The bishop spun around and scooped up some coals throwing them onto the fire. I sat down on the sofa next to Raven and remembered that it was the same noise I had heard during the night. Maybe it wasn't just the third floor that was falling apart. Maybe the chimneys were crumbling down also.

"I do hope I don't have another bird that's got stuck in the chimney," said the bishop, turning to face us. "I've had five already in just this month."

Not overly interested in birds stuck in chimneys, Jude sat down and looked at the bishop. "Do you have a car we could use?"

"I don't drive," answered the bishop. "Never could get the hang of going round all those roundabouts."

"What about Mrs. Gables?" asked Max. "How does she get about?"

"She only has a push bike," said the bishop, taking the armchair by the window. He sat down and stared at the fire. "I'm sorry I can't be of any more help. I know you all want to be on your way but everything happens for a reason – I'm a firm believer in that and maybe the Lord saw fit to keep you all here for another night – maybe He thought we would be much safer."

"So the Lord knifed our tyres, did He?" said Raven, her dark eyes peering through the greasy strands of her hair.

"Like I said, everything happens for a reason. Sometimes we don't always see it at first, and it isn't always clear, but maybe if you had left today then you could have ended up in a worse situation than you are in now," the bishop said, standing up and pulling on the cord which summoned Mrs. Gables.

I leant back against the cushion. I had a mixture of emotions bumping around inside me. On one hand, I felt safe in knowing that having another night here would mean not having to look over my shoulder every couple of minutes for the cleaners, but on the other hand, I was worried that spending too much time here would allow the cleaners to get nearer, making it harder for us to distance ourselves from them when we left. I hated not knowing how close to us they were – it was impossible to gage. I stared into the fire at its hot seething flames and thought of Ben. Where was he? Had he gone back to Cruor Pharma? Had the demon inside him taken over and was now searching the countryside looking for me – wanting another chance to make me beg? Would I see him again? I wanted to. Those guilty feelings I had felt yesterday were now ravaging my insides and fighting against the sensible thoughts I had about staying well clear of him. Those traitorous ideas made me feel bad when I looked at the others. Why couldn't I just shake these emotions away? Why go looking for trouble when I was already stuck in so much already? I closed my eyes. Perhaps it was too late – maybe trouble would come looking for me in the shape of Ben.

CHAPTER TWENTY EIGHT

I woke to the quiet sound of music. Feeling somewhat disorientated, my eyes adjusted to the room and I spotted a small radio placed on a coffee table. It played *It's My Life* by Talk Talk. The room seemed dark and it was only when I looked at a small clock on the mantelpiece that I realised I must have fallen asleep for a good few hours. It was 3:45 and the autumn evening was already drawing in, casting shadows across the room.

I lifted my head from off the cushion and saw Jude standing by the window. He seemed lost in thought as he gazed out. I looked around the room. I wasn't the only one who had fallen asleep. Max lay sprawled out on the other sofa, his eyes shut and his mouth slightly open. I couldn't see Raven. She wasn't in the room. Maybe she was in the bathroom.

"Hey," I whispered, careful not to disturb Max.

Jude turned away from the window and came to sit down next to me.

"You've been asleep for hours," he whispered. "Dream of anything nice?"

I sat and thought for a few moments as I

tried to remember. Fuzzy pictures entered my head as little snippets opened up into larger images.

"Mrs. Gables," I frowned. "She was floating around on fire." I shook my head, feeling a little puzzled. If I could interpret dreams I wondered what that would signify. A sense of sadness came over me. "My dad, I remember him in it." The sadness I had just felt swept away and was replaced with dread as I remembered what my dad had been wearing – a Cruor Pharma uniform. I shuddered. I wasn't sure which image I preferred of my dad. The pissed-up one of him in his armchair surrounded by bottles of whisky or the disturbing one of him, obviously having worked for Doctor Middleton at some time in his life. Neither were great.

"You miss your dad?" whispered Jude, taking hold of my hand. His eyes stared at me intently, like he was trying to see into my mind.

"In a strange kind of way." I shrugged my shoulders. "Although he was always drunk, he was kind of company. I could always tell him anything – my worries, when I was sad, when I'd got into trouble at school. You see, you can tell a drunk anything because they never remember – you can sound off as much as you like, and they'll never tell you off – never judge you. He was good for that but… when you really needed advice, comfort, a shoulder to cry on, and just someone to tell you that everything will be all right… that was when I realised that I was just talking to an empty shell – that I had no one to hear me – I was on my own."

I stared at the fire. It was almost out. Plumes of smouldering smoke whispered up the chimney. The scattering noise came again and I stood up and threw more coals onto the fire. Bits of crumbling brick fell down and I kneeled on the rug and angled my head so I could peer up into the chimney without getting burnt by the flames. Jude came and knelt down beside me screwing up his eyes so he could take a look also.

"Birds?" said Jude. "Sounds more like a freaking ostrich stuck up there."

I laughed at his comment.

"That's the first time I've seen you smile – the first time I've heard you laugh – it's nice." Jude grinned with a smile that lit up his face – made his eyes sparkle and his smooth tanned skin glow with a warmth that I hadn't seen before. I felt a little closer to him even though I didn't really know too much about him – hadn't had long enough to get to know him. Last night had been a start of some kind, and it felt good to have the beginning of a bond between us – a reassurance that we were both playing on the same side. I already felt a connection between me and Max. Stuck in that chapel at Cruor Pharma with Max reading Father Williams's diary with me – we had got on straight away. I hadn't once doubted Max – I trusted him to watch my back and I knew he wasn't the type to do anything stupid – anything that would get us into trouble. So now as I looked at Jude, I felt comfortable believing that Jude was as sincere as Max – not just a guy with sex and booze on his mind – well, almost. His flirty, playboy ways had died down and a more sensible, dependable personality was shining through. It made Jude more appealing to the eye. That just left Raven. I trusted her in a sense that she wasn't a bad person but she made it so difficult to get to know her. She had these walls built around her with tales of ghosts and seeing the dead that it seemed impossible to break through and see the real Raven that was really under there. All I had picked up from her was a life travelling from one place to the next with a mother who happily sent her daughter to be injected with a drug they knew nothing about. It was quite obvious that Raven's mum was more interested in money than her own daughter's welfare. Maybe that explained the walls built around Raven. Maybe that's why she seemed so detached from everyone – she probably never had a chance to build any kind of relationship moving from one place to the next. But weren't we all like that in a way? We seemed to have come from families who were either dead or may as well have been dead. But at least, unlike Raven, we were trying to get along – making an effort to pull in the same direction and get to know a little about each other. I would have to try and be more patient with her, try to break down some of her walls and form some kind of friendship. After all, I had a feeling that we would all be stuck with each other for some time. Maybe even forever.

I looked at Jude. He was still staring at me with that warm smile. I suddenly had the overwhelming need to tell him about my dad. I reached behind me and pulled out the photo of my father that I had found pinned up in the locker room back at Cruor Pharma. It had bothered me ever since finding it and I wanted to unload the burden that had been weighing me down – the uneasy feeling that my dad may have played a part in those terrible drug trials or had known about them and turned a blind eye like all the other staff at Cruor Pharma.

"Look at this," I whispered, handing him the photo.

"Where did you find it?" asked Jude, turning it over in his hand.

"The locker room," I answered. "One of those porters was… my dad." I looked away, unwilling to see Jude's expression. I didn't want to see the look of disgust over his face when he realised that my dad had worked for Doctor Middleton. I felt ashamed and worried that he would think bad of me – think I was a part of all this.

Jude took a deep breath and sighed. "Did you know he worked at Cruor Pharma?"

"No – never had a clue," I said, avoiding his eyes, watching the flames swirl up the chimney.

"Which one is he?" asked Jude.

"That one." I pointed out my dad.

"He never told you anything about it? Never said anything at all?" he asked.

I shook my head. "Never. I don't ever remember him working anywhere. He was always drunk." I took a deep breath and found some courage inside me to face Jude. I couldn't avoid his stare any longer. It was too late to take back what I had confided in him. "The date on the back suggests he must have worked at Cruor Pharma when I was a baby, but from what little information we have found out about Cruor Pharma, what I don't get is why Middleton didn't kill him. Why let him go when he could have been a risk and spoke out about what was happening at the hospital?"

"It seems that your dad had a lucky escape," said Jude, handing me back the photo. "Somehow he managed to slip past Middleton and the others and live the rest of his life or maybe…" Jude stopped mid-sentence.

"Maybe what?" I whispered, searching his eyes for that look of disgust I had been expecting to see. But it wasn't there, just a faint flicker of shadow cast from the fire and the darkening day.

"Maybe they thought they were safe enough, what, with your dad being a pisshead," Jude said.

I flinched at his comment. It hurt. I had said it myself so many times but hearing someone else say it – someone who didn't know my dad hurt – ripped at my heart. I suddenly felt protective over my father.

"He doesn't look like a *pisshead* here though, *does* he?" I snapped, tucking the photo back inside the satchel.

"I guess not," said Jude, completely oblivious that he had hurt my feelings. "So who looked after you while your dad worked at Cruor Pharma?"

"I don't remember... I guess it would have been my mum," I whispered, hating the fact that I really had no idea – that I knew nothing about my mother. It was like searching an empty void – looking into a black hole and just finding nothing. Why had my dad told me so little about her? It seemed impossible to fix the jigsaw when there really weren't very many pieces to play with. I tried to conjure up a timeline in my head. *My dad worked at Cruor Pharma in my first few years and my mum must have been the one who looked after me. Judging by the photo of my dad, he wasn't a drunk then, so what made him turn to the bottle and why did he leave Cruor Pharma?* The only theory I could come up with was that my mum must have died and that's why he left his job to bring me up. Did my dad turn to the bottle because of my mother's death? Or was he trying to drown out something else? Something that he had seen at Cruor Pharma? Well that wouldn't surprise me – I had seen plenty in a short space of time at that place and I certainly felt like having a drink. But why had I always felt like it was because of me that my dad drank himself to unconsciousness? What part did I play in all this? Remembering the things that Carly had said to me when I had been trapped inside that room with her came to the forefront of my mind. She had said some wicked things and what bothered me the most was that some of them were true. But had she been right about what she had said regarding my mother? Had she dumped me? Did my mum want me dead? I crossed my legs and rested my chin on my hands. So many questions had my head spinning – my heart aching.

"Listen, Kassidy," whispered Jude. "Don't hate your dad for working at Cruor Pharma, most people in Holly Tree are employed at that place. Whatever made him turn to the bottle will probably never be discovered. Don't waste your life living under that shadow – leave it in the past. I've left my shadow and I intend on making the most of it – well as soon as we find a way out of the mess we're in." Jude stood up and walked back to the window.

What shadow had Jude left? I could only assume he was talking about his own father and how his dad couldn't be bothered with him. Jude had left his father and I guessed that was his way of leaving the past behind him and escaping the shadow that had hung over his life. But could I really do that? Forget about my parents? I didn't think so. Especially now that I had found out about my dad working for Cruor Pharma and not knowing anything about my mum. It was like an ache – a pain that wouldn't go away. A part of my life was missing and the other half – my dad's half – had been shrouded in a drunken mystery.

I stood up and joined Jude at the window. The cloudy grey sky had turned hazy like a misty lens had been placed over it. The atmosphere outside had changed from the bright autumn sunshine I had stared out upon when I had woken this morning. There almost seemed to be something lingering – something coming. I looked at Jude. Could he feel it too? Was that why he kept coming to the window? Did he have that same feeling that I now felt – a warning – a danger signal – an inner sense that only someone could feel after they had spent time inside Cruor Pharma?

CHAPTER TWENTY NINE

"Have we made the biggest mistake ever by coming here?" I placed my hand on Jude's arm. "Have we been here too long?"

"I don't know," whispered Jude, turning to face me. "But the sooner we get away the better. We can't leave now, it's too late to be wandering around the countryside at night with no car, but I think we should leave at first light – without the car. I know we don't want to leave on foot but I don't think we have the time to go bussing into Rane and then bus back and fix the wheels. I only hope that this bad feeling I've got plays out to be nothing. I hope it's just paranoia that's making me feel on edge." He looked back outside, his eyes wandered from the ash trees to the gravel driveway that twisted away out of sight behind the thick canopy of branches. "We'll leave in the early hours before the bishop or Mrs. Gables wake up. We won't tell them. Let them believe we're catching the bus at 10:30. If it was Mrs. Gables trying to keep us here then I think its best we keep quiet about our real plan – don't you?"

I nodded my head in agreement. We had enough people after us without Mrs. Gables adding to the list.

As if on cue, Mrs. Gables suddenly appeared at the door. Had she heard us? Did she know our true plan of leaving in the early hours? If she did, she didn't let on.

She walked in carrying a tray filled with several plates of sandwiches and jam tarts.

"The bishop won't be eating with you tonight," she glared, placing the tray down onto the coffee table.

"Why, has he gone out?" I asked, staring at her with a matching glare.

"No, he's a busy man and has important work to do," she huffed, taking the plates from the tray and clattering them down on the table. The noise woke Max up. He sat bolt upright as if he'd had an electric shock. His hair was ruffled up like he'd been spinning around in a washing machine.

"How long have I been asleep?" He rubbed his eyes and yawned.

"Long enough to sleep till dinner," answered Jude, taking a sandwich and waving it in front of Max.

"Where's Raven?" he asked, swinging his legs from off the sofa and reaching for a sandwich.

"She huffed off to bed in one of her freaky moods," said Jude, pushing a whole jam tart into his mouth. "She's pissed off because we're staying

257

here another night."

"That little Madame should be grateful she's got somewhere to stay." Mrs. Gables stood in the doorway, her hands on her hips and her narrow cheeks puffed out as she glared at each of us. "The bishop didn't have to take you in, but he did. You should all show some respect for his kindness."

Fearing that there was going to be another argument with Mrs. Gables, I stood up and went to place my hand on her arm. I wanted to smooth things over with her. I didn't want to go to bed later worrying that she was gonna get us in our sleep. I wanted some reassurance that there would be no more trouble from her. Even though we had no firm evidence that it had been her who had slashed the tyres, I strongly suspected that it had been the work of Mrs. Gables.

"Mrs. Gables," I started, "we are very grateful..." My fingers brushed the skin across her hand and she flinched backwards almost toppling over.

"Don't touch me!" she spat, her eyes wide with fear as stared down at my black veins and twisted fingernails.

"It's not catching," I said, pulling my hand away. "You can't get this unless you've been injected with it."

"I know that," snapped Mrs. Gables. "I know it's not some kind of infection. I've seen what it does and I don't want any of you near me when you change…" She took another step away from me.

"What do you mean?" I asked. "Change?"

She shook her head, "I mean… I…"

"What?" I pushed "Tell me."

"I don't have to tell you anything!" she snapped, turning away and hastily leaving the room.

"What the fuck was that about? I really don't get what that woman wants," said Jude. "Either she wants us to stay or she doesn't. Which one is it?"

"What I want to know is what did she mean by us changing?" I said, looking at Jude and Max. "She seems pretty clued up as to what this drug can do to someone."

"Well she would," said Jude, eating another sandwich. "Robert and his lot turned up here – didn't they."

"Yes, but they all left," I said. "The bishop told us they were in a bad way but they all left."

"What are you getting at, Kassidy?" asked Max.

"If they left, they wouldn't have changed –

they would be like us. But if they *had* changed then they would have gone round this house and killed and eaten everyone in it. They would have been like Howard and Wendy." I sat down on the sofa and picked up a ham sandwich. "She's seen one of them change."

"No way," said Jude. "That's not possible. Like you just said – they would have killed the bishop and Mrs. Gables. There's no controlling someone who can't take VA20 or VA10."

"And besides," said Max, leaning forward on the sofa, "how do you explain Sylvia? We know she left here and if she had been the one to change then she would have finished off the bishop and Mrs. Gables before she fled."

"The bishop told us they all headed for Doctor Langstone," said Jude. "There's no reason why he would lie. I just think that Mrs. Gables is one of those people who can't stand others that are different – she's old-fashioned – set in her ways. She's probably one of those busy-bodies you get in a small village who gives a new resident the cold shoulder – thinks of them as strangers."

I took a bite of my sandwich. I wasn't so sure. There had been something in Mrs. Gables's eyes that told me she had seen more than just Robert, Alex, and Sylvia with veins like ours. There had been fear across her face. I remembered the conversation we'd had with the bishop the night before. When Raven had been quizzing him over the state of the others, she had asked him if they had been like zombies and the bishop had said no. So what did Mrs. Gables mean?

I looked over at the window. It was now pitch black outside. I wished for the morning. I had believed that we would find a place of safety here away from the cleaners but now it felt like there was something to fear inside this house. I no longer felt secure, and what worried me more was if I would ever find such a place – somewhere protected – out of harm's way.

CHAPTER THIRTY

Standing in the large hall, the flames in the fireplace seemed smaller. Mrs. Gable's usual inferno was more like a dying campfire. The brass bucket that housed the coals was missing. Maybe she had taken it to refill.

I looked up into the dark void at the top of the staircase and waited for Max or Jude to find a torch. They had wandered off down a narrow hall in the hope that they might find something to light our way upstairs.

We had spent the last few hours sat in the snug. Max and I had taken it in turns to throw on more coals when the scattering noise had sounded over the music that played from the radio. Jude had taken up permanent residence at the window. For someone who had scoffed at the idea of the cleaners and everything paranormal yesterday, he seemed more on edge than the rest of us.

Raven hadn't made an appearance and I guessed she was still sulking upstairs. I had put aside some of Mrs. Gables's sandwiches for her – not that she would probably eat them for fear of being poisoned, but it was the thought that counted.

We hadn't seen or heard the bishop all evening and Mrs. Gables had avoided us since our heated encounter in the snug earlier on. I wondered what kind of work was keeping the bishop up so late. I had poked my head around the door to his study to say goodnight but he hadn't been in there. Maybe he was working up in his bedroom.

Apart from the crackle of the flames, the house was silent. The large hall glowed an eerie shadowy-orange across the stone walls, almost making the pictures on the hanging tapestries come alive.

I was feeling anxious. I wanted to get into our room. I felt vulnerable standing in this hall with its high ceiling and numerous doors leading off in all directions. I didn't like the fact that you couldn't see up past half the staircase or if someone was standing on the landing overlooking the banister into the hall. For all I knew, Mrs. Gables could be up there watching me with her carving knife.

"Don't be silly," I muttered under my breath. I was beginning to sound like Raven. I paced back and forth. My eyes wandered from one door to the next. They looked like black openings concealing dark, ghostly monsters waiting to jump out at me. I tried to ignore them by humming to myself. The sound comforted me – made me feel like I wasn't alone and that this was just any old evening back at my flat where I would be listening to music or watching the T.V.

My humming was cut short when I heard a noise coming from the lounge. I strained my eyes toward the black doorway and listened. My heart had picked up pace and my arms were scattered with goose-bumps. I took a few steps nearer. Silence.

"Enough of this," I scolded myself. "This isn't Cruor Pharma." I headed for the lounge. When I stood in the doorway, I could see nothing but the grey shapes of old furniture and the unused fireplace. I grabbed the handle and pulled the door shut.

"May as well do the rest," I said, heading for the door which led into the dining room. After I had got rid of every dark opening I could, I let out a sigh of relief.

"That's better," I whispered, trying to ignore the darkness at the top of the stairs. I chewed on my lower lip – where the hell had Jude and Max got to? It felt like I had been waiting forever. Just as I was about to start humming again, the sound of footsteps could be heard coming from the narrow hallway. I turned to face it, taking a few steps back – hoping it was my friends and nothing else. I felt my lips turn up into a smile as I spotted Jude and then Max appearing from the darkness. They smiled back at me and waved a candlestick in the air.

"We have light," Max beamed, taking a match from a box and lighting the candle. It did little to brighten the hall but maybe it would work better when we were upstairs finding our way to the bedroom down those dark corridors.

I felt Jude take my hand. "Come on, let's go find our room."

Max led the way. We followed close behind. Each step up the staircase produced a creaky groan. It was impossible to avoid – no matter where you stepped the creaks kept coming.

We reached the top and I felt a huge sense of relief to see that Mrs. Gables wasn't up here slashing her knife about. As we turned left, a rattling noise coming from the other end of the corridor stopped us dead in our tracks. We all turned to face the direction from where it had come. Max came to the back of me and Jude and held up the flickering candle light, illuminating the end of the corridor.

"What's down there?" whispered Max, holding the candle first to the left and then to the right.

"It's another staircase that leads down to the ground floor and goes up to the third floor," I whispered. "I came across it this morning when you were all still asleep."

"Did you go up?" asked Jude.

"Yes, but you can't go any further then the top of the stairs. There's a door which has been padlocked," I said, letting go of Jude's hand and stepping in front of Max. I took another few steps toward the end of the corridor.

"Why tell us not to go up to the third floor when you..." Max begun.

I cut him off. "Shhh...I can hear something." We stood silent and listened. By the time we had realised that it was footsteps it was too late to turn and hide. We all jumped when the bishop appeared at the bottom of the third floor staircase. He looked as shocked to see us as we were to see him.

"My goodness... you gave me a fright," said the bishop, coming toward us.

"We were just going to bed," said Max, holding the candle up so we could see the bishop clearly.

"We heard a noise and wondered what it was," said Jude, eyeing the bishop with a wary gaze. "I thought you said that you didn't use the third floor."

"I... I don't," the bishop smiled. "But I thought I could hear something up there and I checked it out and didn't find anything... probably another bird I suspect. Well... I'll let you all go to bed." He looked down at his hands and brushed them off against his trousers. They were covered in black dirt. He laughed nervously. "It's very dirty up there. Hasn't been cleaned for nearly three months – full of dust. Anyway – goodnight and I'll see you in the morning – oh and make sure you keep those fires burning – there's a real chill in the air tonight" He turned away and disappeared into a room, locking the door behind him.

CHAPTER THIRTY ONE

Raven stood by the dwindling fire in our bedroom. She swung around when she heard us enter. Her face was masked with her usual sulky look. She stood with her hands on her hips, greasy black hair draped over her face like she'd slithered out of the ocean covered in seaweed.

"You're looking good tonight," said Jude, walking straight past her and heading for the window.

"Are we leaving now?" asked Raven, ignoring Jude's bitchy comment.

"Nope," Jude answered, staring out into the dark night.

"Why not?" pushed Raven, glaring at me and Max.

"It's too dark," said Jude, his tone flat like he was bored.

"Get a torch," hissed Raven.

"Don't have one."

"Find one," she sneered.

"You fucking find one," snapped Jude, spinning around to face her.

A loud thump from above made us all look up at the ceiling.

"What has to happen to make you lot leave this house?" Raven said, her eyes still on the ceiling.

"Some daylight, maybe?" said Max, a look of uncertainty across his face as he peered up toward the third floor.

The thump came again and then that scattering noise echoed down the chimney.

"What is that?" I whispered, looking at the others.

"Another ostrich, I guess," said Jude, coming away from the window, only this time there was no jokey tone to his voice. "Look, we're gonna leave as soon as it starts to get a little light. We just need to wait it out here for a couple of hours and then we sneak out."

"What if we don't have a couple of hours?" said Raven, sounding a little pacified now that she knew we would be leaving soon.

Before Jude could reply to Raven, the scattering noise came again but with more force this time. Bits of soot and crumbling brick fell into the hearth. I went to throw more coals onto the fire but there were none left. Mrs. Gables wasn't keeping up with her bonfire obsession in this room.

"There are no coals," I whispered. "I think I'll go get some from the other bedroom." I opened the door and peered out into the corridor. When I was happy that it was empty, I walked over to the other bedroom and pushed open the door. The room was cold. The only light came from the window and that wasn't much. Walking across the bare floorboards, it suddenly dawned on me that the fire had gone out in here. I looked about the hearth for the coals but there were none. The scattering sound came again, only from this chimney instead.

"What the freaking hell is that?" I whispered, getting down on all fours and sticking my head under the chimneybreast. "There can't be birds in every one of these things, surely?" I peered up. It was like staring into a deep, dark cavern. I pulled my head out when a few small clusters of brick fell onto my face. Coughing, I brushed the bits from off my cheeks and stood up. Where could I get some coals? I needed to get this fire going. I shook my head. "God, I'm becoming like Mrs. Gables and her inferno addiction." What did it matter if the fire wasn't burning in here? We weren't sleeping in this room, and if a bird came down – well, that was for the bishop and Mrs. Gables to deal with in the morning. We wouldn't even be here then. I left and shut the door behind me.

"There are no coals," I said to the others as I closed the door to our bedroom.

Before anyone could say anything, a tap on the door made us all spin around. We looked at each other – unsure whether to answer.

"Who is it?" I called out, chewing on my lip.

The door opened and the bishop stepped in. He was dressed for bed in his stripy pyjamas and dressing gown.

"I'm so sorry to disturb you all, but I have a problem and I wonder if you could all help me?" said the bishop. "I know its late but I think some of the old wooden windows have blown open in the wind on the third floor and they need shutting. Do you think you could come up there and help me shut them? I would do it myself but there's quite a few and they will need hammering shut with some nails. The catches and locks no longer work."

"I thought you said it wasn't safe up there?" I questioned.

"It isn't, my dear, but I know where to tread and where to stay away from," smiled the bishop. "I don't know about you four but I need a good night's sleep and those windows thumping open and closed all night is going to keep me awake."

Another loud thump came from above us. I looked round at the others and then back at the bishop's pleading face. He had helped us out by allowing us to stay in his house so it was only right that we returned the favour. Besides, it was probably too much work for the bishop to manage by himself and I couldn't imagine Mrs. Gables up there in the dead of night hammering away.

"I'll give you a hand," said Max, coming to stand beside the bishop.

"Come on then," sighed Jude, looking at Raven and me. "It shouldn't take too long if we all get stuck in."

"Excellent," beamed the bishop, clasping his hands together. "Follow me, and I'll lead the way."

The bishop pulled out a torch and switched it on. The beam of light lit up the corridor as we followed him. Mrs. Gables suddenly appeared in the dark. She was standing at her bedroom door looking meek and timid – her usual act in front of the bishop. If only he knew what she was like when he wasn't around.

"Are you going up to the third floor?" she asked, wringing her hands together. She wore a thick green dressing gown and matching slippers and her head was covered in some kind of bonnet.

"Just fixing those dreadful windows, Mrs. Gables," said the bishop. "Nothing for you to worry about. You go back to bed."

We reached the stairs that led up to the third floor. I looked back down the corridor and watched Mrs. Gables disappear back into her bedroom. She shut the door and I heard her turn the key. The sound of two bolts being slid across echoed through the dark. I was beginning to wonder if Mrs. Gables didn't suffer from a form of OCD, what, with her obsession with lighting fires and locking doors.

"Come on, Kassidy," called Jude. They had already reached the top of the stairs and were now waiting for me.

I climbed two stairs at a time. It was rather cramped at the top and we stood huddled close together while the bishop fumbled with the padlock. His wrinkled old hands trembled as he turned the key.

"There's evil in this house – I can feel it," whispered Raven.

"Don't," said Max, holding up his hand as if to block out Raven's voice. "Don't say that stuff when I'm about to go into some creepy attic."

"Well why did you agree to do it then?" hissed Raven. "You could have said no."

"I don't like the idea of windows open at night when god-knows-what could climb in," whispered Max, turning his back on Raven.

That thought hadn't occurred to me. I had just been happy to return the bishop's help, but now after hearing that from Max, I had horrible images of climbing, freaky things that would sneak in through open windows. I shuddered.

Raven leered out from under her hair. She still had Hannah's jacket zipped up tight to her neck but not enough to cover up the thick black vein that stood out against her pale skin. Her eyes peered down at me and it was then I noticed that cloudy-red haze in them – just like before when we had been hiding in that room after Nurse Jones had been taken. I wondered if my eyes would look like that soon.

"Here we go," whispered the bishop, removing the padlock from the door. "Keep to your right when you go in. I'll hold the torch behind you so you can see where you're treading." His voice trembled as he slowly pushed open the door. Stepping aside, the bishop ushered us in. It was pitch-black and I held my arms out.

"Where are we going?" asked Jude. "You need to shine the torch up front, I can't see a thing."

"Just keep heading straight," hushed the bishop.

I stepped through the door. I was the last

one in except for the bishop who stood behind me waving the torch up and down. I was about to turn around when it dawned on me that there was no wind tonight so how could the thumps be coming from the windows blowing in a breeze that didn't exist? As I opened my mouth to question this, something in the bobbing torchlight made me gasp. I froze to the spot. The small beam of light had moved quickly over the wall and floor but not quick enough to hide an image I had tattooed in my head of the corridors at Cruor Pharma. I spun around. The bishop had already started to close the door on us.

"*No!*" I screamed. "I want to get out!" I hammered my fists against the door and threw all my weight against it. "Jude, don't go any further – it's not safe. We've been tricked! Help me with the door!"

Within an instant, Max was beside me shoving his shoulder through the gap, trying to stop the bishop from fully closing the door. Jude and Raven came up behind us and barged into me and Max – shoving and hurling as much weight as they could to stop the bishop from blocking us in.

"I'm sorry." The bishop's voice came from the other side. "I'm so sorry, but I can't let you leave."

"What happened? What did you see?" shouted Jude over my shoulder as we fought to keep the door open.

"The ceiling…" I yelled. "There's a *bloody handprint* on the ceiling."

CHAPTER THIRTY TWO

The bishop's arm shot through the gap in the door – his hand roughly grabbed at Max's shoulder. His fingers dug into Max's skin as the bishop tried to shove him away from the door.

We piled in tight, as hard as we could within the small confines of the corridor. It was like barging your way onto a packed underground train – desperate to get in first and grab a seat.

For an old man the bishop had some strength. I wanted to get out. I didn't want to be trapped on the third floor with whatever had crawled across the ceiling and left a bloody handprint.

With all the commotion and pushing and shoving, the bishop had dropped the torch and I reached down and grabbed it.

"Mind your head, Max!" I screamed, smashing the torch down over and over onto the bishop's hand that still had hold of Max by the shoulder.

"Open the fucking door now or I'll rip your head off and shove it up your arse!" hollered Jude, shoulder-barging the door.

I heard the bishop gasp as the door must

have hit him in the face. But still he wouldn't let go and continued to try to push Max back.

"Give me the torch!" screamed Raven, snatching at it. "I can hear something." She shone the beam of light down the corridor and it was then I saw the true horror all over the ceiling and walls. It was covered in foot and handprints – bloody and black. The corridor was empty and I swallowed down hard – momentarily relieved that we didn't have anything coming at us from behind. I swung back to face the door.

"Keep the torchlight on the corridor!" I screamed at Raven over the shouts and yells of Max and Jude. Someone had to watch our backs. I lunged down at the bishop's arm and snapped my teeth into his flesh. We had to get him off of Max – weaken him somehow – and if biting down hard into his skin was the answer then I didn't have a problem with that.

The taste of blood filled my mouth and I heard the bishop cry out as I tore a lump of flesh from him. I spat it out and then took another bite. A second cry sounded out from the bishop.

"I'll eat your whole fucking arm if I have to!" I screamed, before clamping my teeth down again and digging my black twisted nails into his flesh.

The bishop let go of Max and I released my

bite. With one hard thrust, Jude and Max flung the door open ramming it into the bishop's face. He lost his balance and toppled over. We all fell out through the open doorway and landed in a heap on top of the bishop.

"*Shut the door,*" shouted Jude. "Lock it... lock it!"

Raven pulled herself up and grabbed the handle, throwing the door shut. With shaky hands she grabbed the padlock and snapped it tight fixing it in place. She spun around and slid slowly down the door until she sat on the floor – out of breath.

A moan came from the bishop as we piled on top of him. We untangled ourselves limb by limb to reveal the bishop lying on the floor – his face pale and scared.

"I'm gonna fucking kill you!" Jude shouted, grabbing the bishop by his throat and pulling him to his feet.

"No... No... please... I'm sorry..." the bishop cried out. "I was scared... I didn't know what to do when you all turned up here at my house... I feared for my life... for Mrs. Gables... I... I..."

"So you thought you'd end ours by locking us up in there with..."Jude started, "...with...who is it you keep in there?"

"Alex... it's Alex..." The bishop shook his

head. His hands trembled like he had been stuck in an artic storm for hours.

I looked at Max, now fearing that his brother, Robert, was dead. As if thinking the same thought as me, Max shoved Jude out of the way and pushed the bishop up against the wall.

"Where's my brother...!? Where's Robert...? If you've killed him, I'll... I'll...," Max stopped. A look of sudden bereavement in his eyes. He swallowed down hard and took a deep breath. "Is he dead?"

"No... I swear it on the Bible... he got away... he escaped," the bishop whimpered. "I tried to lock him up with Sylvia and Alex but he got away with Sylvia and I haven't seen him since."

Max let go of the bishop and turned away. He leant his hand up against the wall and hung his head down, obviously relieved that Robert was still alive.

"Why did you try to lock them up – lock us up?" snapped Jude.

"Don't you mean kill us?" I said, looking at Jude and then at the bishop. "To lock us up would only lead to one thing – our deaths. Anyone put in there with Alex wouldn't last long - not if he's like Howard or Wendy when their bodies couldn't take VA20. And I'm guessing by the blood-stained handprints that that is exactly what Alex is like."

"Call yourself a holy man?" spat Jude. "You ain't ever gonna make it to heaven. There's only one way for you now – down – deep down where the scum exist and their flesh burns slow – you're on a one way ticket to hell."

"Please... I was frightened... I thought if I let you go you would tell Doctor Middleton about me. I was scared I would end up like my priests who knew too much – dead – like Father William and Father Peter." The bishop wiped away a tear that trickled down the wrinkles in his skin. "That's why I said you could all stay here. I wasn't going to lock you up – if you agreed to stay... but Mrs. Gables overheard you talking in the snug about leaving in the early hours. I had to stop you."

"Was it you who slashed our tyres?" hissed Raven.

"Mrs. Gables did it," answered the bishop. "She didn't want any of you here, not after Alex started to change – she was scared that the same would happen to you but she also knew that we couldn't risk letting you leave and giving us up to Doctor Middleton."

I looked over at Max. His Hellraiser T-shirt had been ripped at the shoulder. Everything had started to fall into place now. Mrs. Gables's weird behaviour toward us made sense – the bishop wanting us to stay here with him made sense and now I knew whose T-shirt Max was wearing – it belonged to Alex and the Beyoncé T-shirt was probably his too. But what I didn't understand was why Alex hadn't made an appearance after all the noise we had made on the third floor. Having had some unfortunate experience with people injected with Doctor Middleton's shit, I knew that they didn't sit quiet and behave like normal human beings. They attacked. They killed. So why hadn't Alex done the same?

"We need to leave now," said Jude.

"What about the bishop?" asked Raven. "Don't you think we should lock him up with Alex? And let's not forget Mrs. Gables."

We all turned to look at the bishop. He stood cowering by the wall. His eyebrows and beard were ruffled up even more than usual after our scuffle.

"Please, I beg you... don't put me in there... he's loose... broke out of his chains and now I can't even get in there..." said the bishop. "That's why I keep the third floor padlocked now so he can't get out. I've done everything I can to keep him contained – to keep him quiet. I removed all the lightbulbs upstairs because it seemed to aggravate him. He would scream and wail and go into some kind of frenzy if the lights went on. At first he was easy to manage. We kept him clean and washed his clothes – fed him – but the *change* got worse – he became just too unmanageable – wild."

Before any of us could say anything, the sound of a door could be heard opening. I looked down the staircase. It was pitch-black.

"Mrs. Gables has come out of her room," I whispered. I took a few steps down and listened. I wanted to confront her. I wanted to smile in her face and let her know that her evil plan to lock us up with Alex had failed. But then I remembered Raven's crazy imagination about Mrs. Gables with a kitchen knife. It was dark down there and even though the bishop had failed to lock us up that still didn't mean that Mrs. Gables couldn't have another try at us. She was at an advantage. She knew the layout of this house even in the dark and we didn't. She could jump out at us from anywhere. But there were four of us and only one of her. I looked over my shoulder and beckoned the others to follow me down. We couldn't stay up here all night. We had to leave.

As we reached the bottom of the stairs, Mrs. Gables came tiptoeing out from her room. She was fully dressed with a coat, shoes, and bag.

"Going somewhere nice?" said Jude,

shoving the bishop forward and shining the torch at Mrs. Gables.

"I'm leaving," she muttered. "I can't stay here any longer pretending that it's just me and the bishop who live here. I've had enough babysitting that *thing*." Her eyes stared up at the ceiling. She took a step away from us, slowly edging her way toward the main staircase. "He's all yours now – you can *all* deal with him." Her eyes twinkled in the torchlight as she gripped the top of the banister.

"Mrs. Gables, you can't leave me here alone to deal with Alex – how will I ever manage him by myself?" The bishop stepped forward and held out his hands. "Please... we can think of something... we could..."

"You won't need to worry about dealing with Alex," spat Mrs. Gables. "He'll deal with you – *all* of you." She turned and walked down the staircase.

"What do you mean?" asked the bishop, his eyes looked down upon the dark hall – it was pitch-black. "What have you done...?" He gasped and threw his hands up to his face with a look of shock – or was it sheer terror that appeared in his eyes?

"What the fuck does it matter if the old bag leaves?" snapped Jude, "Who gives a shit?"

"Dear God." The bishop closed his eyes and

shook his head.

"Now ain't the time to stand and pray!" yelled Jude. "She's leaving – so what – we're leaving too."

"The fires... she's put them out... help me get them started..." the bishop flew down the stairs. Reaching the fireplace, he turned to Mrs. Gables as she unlocked the front door. "Where are the coals... they've gone... where have you put them?"

"There are none." Mrs Gable's cold stare appeared in the slither of moonlight that seeped through the gap in the door. Stepping out, she slammed the front door shut. The clank of a key turning filled the large hall with an echo.

"She's locked us in," hissed Raven.

"We need to get the fires going..." shouted the bishop.

"Why...? What is it with these fires?" I snapped, watching the bishop frantically crawl around on his hands and knees in search of some coal.

He looked up at me, his face pale. "When the fire goes out... Alex comes out."

CHAPTER THIRTY THREE

"He climbs down the chimneys." The bishop stood up and looked about the large hall. "The third floor has several fireplaces and they all have access to different rooms in the house."

"Shit," whispered Max, looking over his shoulder.

"If we light the fires then we can stop him," said the bishop, turning away.

"Wait," I whispered. "He's already in the house." That was why he hadn't appeared when we had struggled up on the third floor. He had already climbed down one of the chimneybreasts. But which one?

"What?" Max took a step nearer until he stood right in front of me. "How do you know?" His eyes grew wide with fear as he stared into my face, his voice little more than a whisper. "Please don't tell me he's right behind me?"

I was about to answer him when the sound of scattering came from the fireplace. We stepped away – all of us. Small bits of brick dropped out from the inside of the chimneybreast and tumbled onto the stone floor.

Jude held up the torch and shone it at the

fireplace. I felt the hairs on the back of my neck stand up when a low, guttural moan came from the darkness of the chimneybreast.

The bishop grabbed Jude's arm and yanked it down. "Don't shine the light – he doesn't like it."

"Let's get out of here." Jude headed for the front door. He gripped the handle in his fists and pulled with all his strength. It wouldn't budge. Max joined him and began to kick at the door. It was pointless – we weren't ever going to get out that way.

"Upstairs!" shouted the bishop. "Is the fire still going in your bedroom?" He headed for the staircase.

"I don't know, it was beginning to die down but I couldn't find any more coal," I said, chasing the bishop up the stairs. Raven followed close behind – Jude and Max at her heels.

"Why are we even going with him?" asked Raven. "He lied to us and tried to get us killed. He could be leading us into another trap."

The bishop swung around at the top of the stairs and looked at us. "Alex is on the loose – I need you and you need me – if we are to get out of this mess unharmed. I can't contain Alex by myself, and besides, we can't get out of the house. Mrs. Gables has probably taken all the keys. We're trapped in this together."

He turned away and continued to head toward our bedroom.

"What should we do?" I asked the others. "Do we follow him?"

A noise from the hall downstairs echoed up through the dark – like something had fallen.

"I don't think we've got time to stand here and debate it." Max started to shove us down the corridor. "Go – go!" He looked over his shoulder as the sound of feet slapping on the stone slabs of the hall became louder – nearer.

I didn't need any persuading. I ran. It wouldn't take Alex long to reach us. I remembered how fast the volunteers back at Cruor Pharma had moved, how they had crawled along walls and their ability to clamber over ceilings. I took a sharp right and caught sight of the bishop in the dark disappearing into our bedroom. Panic rose up inside me as I heard another low moan seep down the corridor. With long strides, I reached the bedroom and flew in, almost knocking the bishop off his feet. I turned to see Raven, Jude, and then Max pile in and slam the door shut.

"Block it!" I shouted, grabbing hold of the end of the bed and pulling it across the floorboards.

Max and Jude held the door. The bishop took hold of the other bed and began to slide it over.

"Hurry up!" yelled Raven as she helped me push the bed against the door. Jude and Max climbed on and continued to push all their weight against the door while the bishop and I heaved the other bed on top of the first one.

I stepped away from the piled-up beds and looked for anything else we could use. There was nothing. Just the wooden rocking chair.

"The fire is almost out," said Jude, leaning against the bed. "Now what are we gonna do?"

The bishop bent down and began to stoke up the coals with a long brass fork. It was pointless. What little coals were left were barely glowing. There were no flames. Just wispy tendrils of smoke.

"Try the window!" shouted Jude, still holding the beds in place.

Raven yanked at the window latch but it wouldn't budge. "It's locked," she hissed, "The panes of glass are too small to climb through even if we could smash them."

I looked out into the night. The ground below was too far down for us to jump even if we could get the window open, but I knew if it came to it, I would rather jump than take the option of fighting Alex.

"Well," said Jude, glaring at the bishop. "This is your place and your mess – how are you gonna get us out of here?"

A loud bang against the door almost knocked Jude over. Alex was outside. The bang came again, followed by what sounded like snarling and groaning. Max and Raven pushed themselves up against the beds.

The bishop closed his eyes for a few moments like he was lost in deep thought. His eyebrows twitched on his face. Letting out a slow sigh, he said, "The chimney."

"What?" Are you mad?" I snapped. "We can't climb up chimneys."

"It's the only way out of this room," he whispered. "If we can get up this chimney, it will take us up to the third floor."

"Then what?" hissed Raven. "We trap ourselves up there and wait for that devil's spawn to get us?"

"There are other chimneybreasts we could then climb down," whispered the bishop, pacing back and forth. "If we take the one that leads down into the lounge, we could get out through the front windows. The frames are weak – rotten – it wouldn't take much to break them."

"Wouldn't it have made more sense to have gone to the lounge in the first place then?" snapped Raven. "Why drag us all up here?"

"I just thought that if we got all the fires going and maybe trapped Alex somehow then all this dreadful mess could have been contained," answered the bishop.

"Let's just open the door and get him," said Jude. "There's only one of him and five of us – we can do it."

"No!" I shouted, just the thought of even seeing Alex petrified me – filled my head with images of Howard pulling himself across the floor on Ward 2 with his innards all hanging out. I didn't want to face such sights ever again, let alone have to roll around on the floor and fight Alex.

"Don't open the door," warned the bishop. "He's way beyond being controlled. His strength is unbelievable. If we're going to trap him then we need to approach him from behind – take him by surprise."

I chewed on my lip and paced back and forth like the bishop. What should we do? My heart pounded away inside my chest and I cursed myself for not being more vigilant toward the bishop and Mrs. Gables. How they had been insistent about keeping the fires burning and the weird scattering noises coming from the chimneys. I had been more concerned about fearing the outside – the cleaners and the police, to even think that I should be watching my back inside the bishop's home.

"Confront Alex or take the chimney?" Jude cut into my thoughts.

"Why risk getting killed by Alex, when there's a way out through the chimney?" asked Max. "I know it's not ideal, but…" He broke his sentence and looked at me. "We've got this far and I know it's all turned to shit but… we can do this… we can get out of here."

I looked at the chimney. The sudden smash against the door made me jump. The wood panelling buckled and the beds rocked and jolted. It was obvious that we wouldn't be able to hold back Alex for much longer. I didn't want my life to end here or anywhere, and I didn't want to see either of my friends get killed. I had seen enough death.

I snatched up Father Williams's satchel and reluctantly walked over to the fireplace. "Let's take the chimney." I got down on all fours and peered up into the dark cavity.

CHAPTER THIRTY FOUR

With the smouldering embers now out, I climbed up into the chimney. It was like a narrow tunnel filled with nothing but an endless black space. My knees and elbows scraped against the rough, sooty brick as I tried to propel myself up. It was slow-going but the loud thuds and bangs coming from the bedroom door kept me moving. I had my eyes half shut as brick and soot crumbled down upon my face. Max climbed in behind me. I could hear his shallow gasps as he pulled himself up. Right now, I didn't know what was worse. Trapped inside Cruor Pharma or struggling to get up this goddamn chimney with Alex lurking close by in the darkness? I paused, just for a second and tried to regain my breath. My muscles hurt and my throat felt thick with soot. How much further did I have to go before I reached the third floor? I felt like I was suffocating.

"Keep moving." The muffled voice of Raven filtered up. *She must be below Max,* I thought. I started up again – shinning my way up the chimney like a caterpillar. Just when I thought I would never break free from the constricting tomb-like tunnel, my hands found a break in the chimney. Spurred on by the sudden find and the longing to be free, I found the strength in my arms to pull myself up into a small fireplace. I crawled out, scattering tiny clumps of coal and brick with me. I took large gulps of air before turning around and helping Max as his head appeared in the gloom of the fireplace.

He grasped my hands and pulled himself out. "Raven's coming next," he said, clearing his throat.

We knelt down and grabbed Raven by her wrists, yanking her up and out of the chimney. As she cleared the fireplace, a yell came from down below. It was the bishop.

"He's coming, he's coming!" the bishop shrieked.

Leaning over in the dark void from where we had climbed, Max and I could just make out the top of Jude's head. I breathed a sigh of relief that he was next and not the bishop.

"Come on, Jude," I urged him on. That nervous panic was rising within me.

"Hurry... hurry," called the bishop, his voice full of fear.

Jude scrambled free of the chimney just as the cries of the bishop sounded out.

"He's got me... He's got my ankles...*help!*" the bishop screamed. The sound of his cries and the noise of his body falling back down the chimney echoed up to the third floor. I pulled away from the fireplace not wanting to hear the sickening sound of the bishop's flesh being torn from his body.

"Block the chimney up," Jude said, grabbing hold of what looked like several old suitcases. He pushed them down into the opening of the chimney, wedging them tight so Alex couldn't climb out. "Don't know how long that will hold him back but let's not wait around to find out." He headed across the shadowy attic toward a door.

"We need to stay as quiet as possible," whispered Max. "Remember, Alex is still roaming around down there and he's got access to other chimneys. He could climb up here within minutes."

"We don't know which chimney to take," hissed Raven, spinning around and looking through the dark. "How will we know which one of these fireplaces leads down to the lounge?"

"Fuck knows." Jude shrugged his shoulders and quietly opened the door.

"There's nothing out here except that corridor we were in earlier where the bishop tried to lock us in," whispered Max, peering over Jude's shoulder. "I guess we need to pick a chimney and pray it's the right one."

As my eyes adjusted to the dark attic, I could see we were in the roof of the house with its vaulted ceiling and old wooden beams. The attic was huge and I guessed this would have been the servant's quarters many years ago. The air smelt of damp and rot, and as I looked down at the floor I could see bloody handprints all over it.

"How many fireplaces can you count?" I whispered, struggling to see much further from where I stood.

Jude disappeared into the gloom of the attic and came back within moments. "Six. I think we should pick the biggest," he whispered. "It might be the one that leads down into the lounge or the main hall. Either one will do."

We stood huddled together in the centre of the attic. I kept my eyes on the fireplace that we had just climbed – fearful that Alex would try to climb out. I listened but the only noise I could hear was from our own heavy breathing and the creaks of the floorboards.

"Take that big one," hissed Raven, pointing at the largest fireplace. "I'm not going down the smaller ones – I'll get stuck and die of suffocation."

"Let's go then," whispered Max. "Use your arms and knees to support you as you go down – there won't be anything to grip onto." He headed over to the fireplace at speed.

Raven peered through the dark at me. Her face was covered in black soot and her hair looked like she'd had a bucket of tar poured over it. She really did look like a swamp monster.

"Don't go slipping down that chimney," she mumbled. "You're no good dead. Maybe I should go before you – if you slip then I'll break your fall."

"What about you?" I whispered, surprised by her suggestion. "What if *you* fall?"

"I won't," she hissed. "I'm good at climbing."

I followed her over to the hearth and got down on my hands and knees. I felt sick. I really didn't want to go back inside another chimney, especially this one. It was longer than the one we had just climbed up. My stomach churned at the thought that we could get halfway down and Alex could suddenly appear from either end. Then what would we do? It would be a race to get out before he caught us, and a chimney was no place to race.

"You two go first," said Jude, crouching down beside the hearth. "When you get to the bottom – wherever it comes out – head for the lounge and get those windows open. Don't wait for anyone – just go."

Raven had already started to disappear

down the chimney with just the top of her head poking out. I looked at Jude. His blue eyes almost seemed to pierce through the dark. He looked at me and winked.

"What if one of us gets stuck?" I whispered.

"I'll be right above you," he said. "If you get stuck then I'll get stuck with you – now go." He stroked the side of my face and ushered me into the chimney.

I was just about to lever myself down when movement in one of the other fireplaces caught my eye. I froze.

"What is it – what's wrong?" whispered Max, his eyes narrowed.

"The fireplace... look..." My heart beat so hard I thought it would explode. "Alex is coming out of the chimney."

CHAPTER THIRTY FIVE

Alex appeared in the fireplace. Just his head and one arm at first. His long fingers snatched at the air like spiders legs and he gnashed his teeth together and snarled when he saw us. The sight of us seemed to excite him as he thrashed around, half in–half out of the chimney. I could hear his teeth snapping together along with his laboured breathing. It sounded like his lungs were full of liquid.

"Go, Kassidy... go!" shouted Jude, pushing down on my head – the lower half of my body hanging precariously down the chimney.

I didn't need any persuasion. The sight of Alex and his snapping jaws had my body pumping with adrenaline. There was no way I was gonna hang around. I only prayed that Jude and Max would make it down into the chimney and reach the bottom before Alex could crawl in and get them both.

As I disappeared down into the chimney, I wedged myself against the brickwork and shimmied further down using the same method I had done in the other chimney – like a caterpillar – only this time I moved faster. There was more room in this chimney, which was good, but it was also more dangerous – easier to slip and fall.

I peered down into the dark. I couldn't see Raven but I could hear her clambering down. Looking up, I could see Jude lowering himself into the chimney. I continued to move down. Father Williams's satchel scraped against the brickwork sending clusters of soot and rubble tumbling below.

"Keep moving!" yelled Jude. His feet were just above my head.

"Is Max in here?" I breathed, fearful that he hadn't made it in.

"He's right above my head." Jude's voice echoed past me.

"Speed up!" shouted Max.

I could hear the panic in his voice. If Alex got into the chimney then it would be Max who would be the first to die. I continued to move my body down – top half bent forward – lower half-knees up. It felt like I'd been stuck in the chimney forever. We had to be halfway down by now – didn't we?

"Raven," I called. "Are you at the bottom?"

"Not yet." Her voice sounded muffled. "But I can see it."

"Move. Move!" Max's voice filled the

chimney. "He's climbing in, I can hear him."

I panicked. Fear gripped my insides at the thought of Alex scuttling down the chimney. I lost concentration. I slipped and fell. I blindly flung my arms and legs out – the skin on my hands grated against the bricks. My stomach turned upside down as I continued to drop – like I was falling on a bungee-rope. I hit something – a small bend in the chimney. It was enough to break my fall and allow me to regain myself. Stunned, I continued to edge myself down. I felt shaken and dazed. The fall had scared me but not as much as the low-pitch wails coming from Alex above. I breathed a shaky sigh of relief when my feet touched ground. The fall, although frightening, had helped me reach the bottom of the chimney faster. Collapsing to my knees, I crawled out from the fireplace and found myself in the large hall. Somewhat disorientated, I stood and tried to find my bearings. My heart pumped loud in my ears and my legs felt like they wanted to buckle. My eyes spotted the door to the lounge and I ran toward it.

"Raven... I'm here..." Suddenly I was snatched up. My feet left the floor. My back hurtled against the ceiling of the hall, my body pinned to the plaster. I gasped at the sight of Ben. He hung below me – horizontal to my body. It was like we were lying down on the ceiling – me facing the floor and Ben facing me.

"What… what…" was all I could stutter? Ben pressed his body tight to mine and pushed his finger against my lips.

"Shhh," he hushed. "The police are outside."

I could feel myself tremble. I was pinned to the ceiling – Alex was after me – the bishop had tried to kill me, and now the police were outside. My head swam. My breathing juddered like an old car engine.

"I have to tell the others," I whispered, my voice cracked as I stared down at the floor. My body stiffened. Ben held me firm, his hands gripped tight about my wrists – his feet locked against mine keeping me pinned flat to the ceiling.

A loud scuffle came from the fireplace. Jude clambered out with Max close behind. I opened my mouth to warn them about the police but Ben suddenly pushed his lips against mine – stopping me from making a sound. I could feel the rough of his stubble against my skin. His lips parted from mine as Raven called out from the lounge.

"The police are here." She ran out into the hall.

"Shit," said Jude. "Where's Kassidy?" I

302

watched him spin around as he looked for me.

"I don't know," hissed Raven. "What about Alex?"

In their blind panic, I watched as they hesitated – unsure which direction they should go.

"Kassidy – Kassidy," Max called out. "We can't leave her in here."

I looked into Ben's black eyes. "I have to go to them… they're my friends… please," I whispered.

He shook his head. "I'll drop you… if you call out… I'll let you go."

Before I could plead any more with him, the scattering sound that I had heard so much of since arriving at Dusk Fall Retreat echoed out from the chimney. A pile of brick and soot tumbled out across the floor. Alex appeared.

CHAPTER THIRTY SIX

Gasping, I watched Jude, Max, and Raven scatter. They fled toward the dining room. Alex scuttled across the floor after them. His body was emaciated and covered in large black and purple bruises. Every vein in his body looked as though it had burst under the skin. I struggled against Ben. He didn't budge.

"Drop me then," I snapped. "I don't care. I want to be with my friends. They need my help."

"Do you want me to help them?" Ben's eyes peered at me like two deep, black wells – a tiny ripple babbled over them – like a glimmer of amusement.

"Yes," I snapped, trying to pull my arms away from the ceiling – it was like they were glued to the spot.

"Are you going to beg me?" he whispered before kissing my neck.

To beg him was the last thing I wanted to do but when I looked down, I could see Alex hurling himself against the dining room door desperate to get at my friends.

"Well...?" Ben smiled, a tiny wave of blue bobbed across the black sea in his eyes.

Alex threw himself against the door and I could see through the dark that it was beginning to buckle against his weight.

"I'm waiting, Kassidy." Ben's teeth nipped at my ear.

"Yes..." I hissed through gritted teeth. "Yes... I'm begging you, okay? See...I've done it..."

Ben smiled.

A loud bang came from the front door. It echoed up through the hall. Alex stopped in his tracks and spun around, his attention momentarily taken off my friends.

"Shall I let the police in?" smiled Ben, pushing his body tighter against mine.

I knew what his intention was. I nodded my head.

The front door flew open, almost falling from its hinges. Six police officers piled in, obviously expecting to find me and my friends. But instead they were faced with Alex.

I held my breath. More blood was about to be shed and I closed my eyes to the sight of the bloody murder. The hall was filled with screams and cries. I opened one eye. The floor was like a sea of blood with body parts scattered over it. It was like the aftermath of a plane crash in the sea. I could hear bones snapping and flesh being ripped and torn. Four of the six officers lay scattered in bits across the stone slabs. Alex moved like lightning – a wild animal catching his prey – an endless torrent of slaying.

"Get outta here!" The officer cried to his colleague as Alex turned his attention to them.

Even though the police were a part of all this, I watched, willing them on – wanting them to make it out the front door and escape from Alex. I wanted to scream at them to run – to run for their lives but I didn't. I knew that if I made a noise then Alex would turn his attention on me. I gasped as both officers slipped and stumbled through the sloshy mess, their goal to make it out the door and escape. Alex sprang to his feet. He hurled himself up onto the wall and scuttled at speed, swooping his arm low and snatching up both officers by their hair. They screamed. Alex threw them down – their bodies smashed onto the stone slabs. I watched as Alex flung himself from off the wall. He landed on top of the officers and quickly set about ripping open one of their chests – burying his head into the cavity and tugging with his teeth on the innards. He moved onto the last police officer who was trapped under the body of his dead colleague.

"No… no… please!" the officer screamed. I closed my eyes as Alex began to stamp on the officer's head. I didn't want to see it. I couldn't bear anymore. Something wet splattered up onto my face as the hall was filled with the sound of breaking bones and a slushy kind of popping noise.

Ben's body shuddered against mine and I opened one eye and looked at him. He was laughing quietly.

I wanted to wipe my face. I could feel lumps of flesh – bits of brain – stuck to my lips. I tried to spit them away. My eyes slowly rolled over the sight below – eyelashes clumped together with jelly-like clots of bloodied tissue. The stone slabs were like a crimson carpet. Alex lay on his stomach, thrusting a severed hand into his mouth. The fingers flapped about as he tried to gulp the hand down.

I heaved.

"There's someone else who needs to be dealt with," Ben smiled.

"Who?" I swallowed hard.

"Look," Ben turned his head toward the snug. The bishop's body was dragged out into the hall – appearing to move by itself.

"No... please," the bishop cried out when he saw Alex covered in blood.

"I thought he was dead... I ..." Clenching my fists, I tried to loosen the grip that Ben had on my wrists. "Alex will kill him."

"And?" hushed Ben.

"He doesn't need to die... he..." I shut my eyes as Alex started to crawl toward the bishop. He choked out a garbled laugh.

"He tried to kill you... he was going to send you down the chimney into the lounge," glared Ben. "That chimney's boarded up. You would have been trapped inside it."

Ben was right. I remembered now how I had peered up into the chimneybreast on the first day we had arrived here. I shuddered at the thought. The bishop had tried to kill us twice.

"Please... someone help me..." the bishop cried out.

"Well...?" whispered Ben. "Doesn't he deserve to die?"

I closed my eyes as Alex lunged forward, taking the bishop by the throat. I cringed at the sound of his neck snapping and the noise of Alex's teeth brutally crunching into bone.

"You... you were meant to help me..." Alex starred down at the bishop's dead corpse. A loud wail echoed through the hall as Alex clutched his knees up to his chest and rocked back and forth. A mixture of emotions suddenly shot through me. I was stunned to hear him speak. To me, he had seemed like a crazy, out of control monster. I hadn't once expected him to be able to talk – to still feel – to understand what was happening. My heart ached. Although a killer – none of this was his fault. He was trapped inside a body and mind that was slowly dying – infected. This young guy had once been like Jude and Max but now... now...? Was there any helping him? I looked into Ben's black eyes and whispered, "Can anything be done to save him?"

Ben shook his head slowly and murmured, "He's too far gone."

"Put him out of his misery then." I blinked back tears. "He shouldn't be left to suffer."

"I like watching people suffer," glared Ben. His face had clouded over with a dark shadow.

"Well I don't," I hissed. "Do it."

Ben dropped to the floor leaving me still, somehow, pinned to the ceiling. Expecting Alex to lunge at Ben, I was surprised to see him cower away.

"Help me... you can... help... me..." Alex held up both arms like a toddler reaching for his mum. "You're a part of me... I have... you in me..." He knelt up – his fingers snatched at the air – his black twisted nails clattering together.

I watched as Ben pulled Alex up and held

him by the neck in an arm lock.

For the first time I could see Alex's face clearly. His bloodshot eyes peered up at the ceiling. The skin on his face was hanging in large shreds and his lips had rotted away. He snarled up at me and tried to pull free from Ben.

Suddenly, the sound of bells could be heard. They jingled through the hall sending goose bumps racing across my skin. They were the bells that chimed when the bishop pulled on the cords for Mrs. Gables. But who was left in the house to pull them – all of them? The radio in the snug suddenly burst into life playing *Toy soldiers* by Martika. I looked at Ben. But he seemed as surprised as I was. My heart thumped in my chest. Something shadowy seemed to glide across the hall toward Ben. It wasn't a cleaner; there was more form to its shape but not enough to tell who it was.

"What are you doing here?" its voice rasped.

"Cleaning up the mess you've made," snarled Ben, still holding Alex tight.

"We don't need you," hissed the shadowy form. I couldn't tell if it were male or female – its voice was distorted - almost like static – stuck between two radio stations – unable to tune itself in.

"I think you do," glared Ben. "I guess you're still keeping up with the pretence. She'll find out."

"Do you even have any idea who she is?" The dark form took a step closer to Ben.

"Sssshhhh." Ben's eyes peered up at me.

Who were they talking about – me? I watched as the shadowy form appeared to look up toward me. The radio suddenly turned up full blast and I strained to hear what Ben was saying. I squinted my eyes as I tried to lip-read but it was no use. Then as fast as the dark shape had appeared it vanished – melting away into nothing.

"Who was that?" I shouted at Ben. He ignored me, and then taking Alex by the hair with one hand and the other around his neck, he twisted Alex's head with one quick wrench. I screwed my eyes shut, wishing that I could move my hands so I could stick my fingers in my ears and block out the terrible sound of splintering bones. When the hall had fallen silent, I opened my eyes. Ben dropped what was left of Alex to the floor and calmly walked over to the dining room. Kicking it open, he looked inside, then turned away and gazed up at me.

"Are you gonna stay up there all night?" his lips twisted up into a grin.

"I can hardly get down by myself," I

snapped.

"You could if you really tried," said Ben, brushing down his trousers and waistcoat.

"Yeah, if I want to just drop to the floor and break all my bones," I glared down at him.

"Suit yourself," he shrugged, rolling down the sleeves of his white shirt. "But a little practice and you'll soon be crawling across walls and ceilings."

"What do you mean?" I asked. Was he trying to tell me that I was going to turn into something like Alex?

"You've got a bit of demon in you – that's all I'm saying." He jumped up, springing through the dark, pinning his body to mine. "Shall we go?"

"Where?"

"We need to find your friends. The cleaners are coming." He slipped his arms around me, and before I could blink, my feet were already on the floor.

"Mind you don't slip," whispered Ben, stepping between the puddles of blood and body parts.

I followed him across the hall to the front door, jumping between the bodies like I was on stepping stones. Should I even go with him? He was one of the six demons that the bishop had told us about. Could I trust him? How did I know that he wasn't trying to lure me and my friends together so he could gain control of the cleaners? But he had just stopped me from getting killed by Alex and getting taken away by the police. He had helped me get away from Cruor Pharma. But that could be for his own gain – not because he truly wanted to help me or cared about me.

I hesitated by the front door. Peering back over my shoulder, I looked at the bloody carnage spread across the stone slabs of the hall. There was nothing here for me. There was no reason to stay, and besides, the cleaners were coming. For now, I would take my chances with Ben and his demon. And if I were being honest with myself, there was a part of me that wanted to be with him. Demon or not – one of them had got under my skin and I couldn't shake those feelings off. I would find the others and then we would head north – to Doctor Langstone's. I had so much to find out and I intended to get my answers from Ben. No one else was gonna give them to me. I had no idea how long Ben would stay. Would he go back to Cruor Pharma – would the demon in him drag him away, or would Ben be strong enough to resist him? From what I had seen inside the bishop's home, the demon had prevailed – reigned over Ben.

I took a step outside. The early hours of the morning were filling up with fog, a sight that only reminded me of being at the top of Strangers Hill. I shuddered. Ben turned to face me, his eyes were still black but his face had lost that dark shadow.

Taking my hand and smiling at me, Ben, or was it his demon, led me out into the night.

'Demon'

(Kassidy Bell Series)
Book Three
Coming Soon!

To connect with Lynda O'Rourke visit her facebook
page at:
LyndaO'Rourkefacebook

15393103R00179

Printed in Poland
by Amazon Fulfillment
Poland Sp. z o.o., Wrocław